Kiss and Make Up
DIARY ❤F
A CRUSH

Kiss and Make Up
DIARY ♥OF A CRUSH

SARRA MANNING

www.atombooks.net

ATOM

Written by Sarra Manning and based on
the *J17* column *Diary of a Crush*

First published in Great Britain in 2004 by Hodder Children's Books
This paperback edition published in 2013 by Atom

Copyright © 2004 by Sarra Manning

The moral right of the author has been asserted.

*All characters and events in this publication, other than
those clearly in the public domain, are fictitious and any resemblance
to real persons, living or dead, is purely coincidental.*

All rights reserved.
No part of this publication may be reproduced, stored in a
retrieval system, or transmitted, in any form or by any means, without
the prior permission in writing of the publisher, nor be otherwise circulated
in any form of binding or cover other than that in which it is published
and without a similar condition including this condition being
imposed on the subsequent purchaser.

A CIP catalogue record for this book
is available from the British Library.

ISBN 978-0-349-00157-9

Printed and bound in Great Britain by
Clays Ltd, St Ives plc

Papers used by Atom are from well-managed forests
and other responsible sources.

MIX
Paper from
responsible sources
FSC® C104740

Atom
An imprint of
Little, Brown Book Group
100 Victoria Embankment
London EC4Y 0DY

An Hachette UK Company
www.hachette.co.uk

www.atombooks.net

Acknowledgements

Thanks to Ally Oliver, my editor at *J17*, who commissioned me to write the *Diary of a Crush* as a monthly column and her successor, Sophie Wilson, for continuing to commission me to write *Diary of a Crush*.

I would also like to thank Emily Thomas for giving me my first proper book deal after reading *Diary of a Crush*, my agent Karolina Sutton for working so hard and tirelessly on my behalf and Samantha Smith, Kate Agar and all at Atom for giving these books a shiny, new home.

Finally, I'd like to thank all the readers of *Diary of a Crush*. From the *J17* days, to the people who bought the books first time round, to you (yes YOU!) discovering Dylan and Edie for the first time. What a long, strange trip it's been.

Dedicated to the late, great, never out of date Gordon and Regina Shaw, who put up with me when I was a teenager.

Note to future biographer

In the faint hope that I become a great British novelist by the time I'm twenty-five but die young and tragically, you'll probably be sifting through these diaries for the good of future generations.

Problem is, I've hidden the diary before this, away from my mother's prying eyes, and can't actually remember where I put it. So I'll just give you the greatest hits:

- *Moved to Manchester.*
- *Started at college to do my A-levels and had, like, no friends.*
- *Fell in love with a moody art boy called Dylan on day two of new college.*
- *Am now best friends with his best friend since toddlerdom, Shona.*
- *Am deadly enemies with Mia, Dylan's former and very evil ex who also got her talons into Paul, Shona's ex boyfriend, 'cept they're back together again. Do keep up.*
- *After months and months of many passionate kisses and*

Dylan acting like a complete jerk immediately afterwards, we went on a college trip to Paris and ended up together. As a couple. Boyfriend and girlfriend.

- *My hair is a lot blonder now than it was in this previously-mentioned diary. Because I'm like, worth it.*

Edie's Journal
Manchester

8th April

I have this photograph of me and Dylan tucked into my diary. We're standing on the deck of the ferry on our way back from France in a force-ten gale, so his tufty dark brown hair is even more dishevelled than usual. Dylan's got his arm around my shoulders and he's squinting down at me and smiling fondly like I'm the greatest thing in the world. Even greater than our recent discovery that chopping up chocolate chip cookies and scooping them into vanilla ice cream will give you twice the sugar rush you normally get from eating them straight.

He certainly looks happy to be my boyfriend.

But over the last week I've made the startling discovery that having a boyfriend is nothing like I imagined. No. Scratch that. Having Dylan as a boyfriend is *exactly* how I imagined it. Or thought it might be in my worst nightmares.

All that stuff he came out with on the boat about

how being boyfriend and girlfriend was going to be like we were before but even better? And we'd hang out with each other like we used to but there'd be all this amazing kissing and touching and, I don't know, boyfriendly behaviour? Well, not so much.

Because now that Dylan's my boyfriend, I have to handle his weirdness head-on. His weirdness has, like, rules. Not that he's given me a written list but if he did, it would go something like this:

1. Don't ever come round to my house. Ever.
2. Don't hold hands with me in public.
3. Kissing and touching and boyfriendly behaviour should be restricted to dark corners.
4. Pet names are prohibited.
5. Don't expect me to call when I say I will or be on time for anything or come round for Sunday lunch with your parents.

Some of it is good. A lot of it is good. And my kissing technique has drastically improved with all the extra practice I'm getting but Dylan was way more affectionate when we were bickering mates.

9th April
I was sitting by the piddly college fountain with Shona when Dylan sauntered over to us.

'God, Edie,' Shona muttered when she caught sight

of Dylan, 'you can't be planning to go off and make out *again*. You look like you've had collagen lip implants as it is.'

'Shut up,' I said plaintively. 'You make me feel like I'm just a big kiss slut.'

She arched an eyebrow. 'Oh, I must be getting you confused with someone else then.'

Then Dylan was there. 'Which hand?' he drawled, putting his arms behind his back. My heart leapt. Had he bought me a present?

'The left?'

Dylan gave me a huge, sunshiney grin. 'That was the right answer,' he said, swinging a key in front of my eyes.

'What's that?' I asked, though it was pretty obvious what it was, but I felt like I needed more details.

'It's the key to the darkroom. You coming?'

'Who said romance was dead?' I heard Shona hiss to no-one in particular as I jumped off the wall and followed Dylan in the direction of the art block.

I had been planning to tell Dylan a few truths, I really had, but once we got into the darkroom he immediately reached for me and I kind of forgot. Dylan had me wedged against the enlarger so I couldn't move but I didn't want to. I felt sort of boneless and lethargic like Pudding does when she's all sleepy and lying in the sun. Dylan's tongue was causing havoc everywhere it went when we were suddenly interrupted by the door banging open.

'Sod off,' snarled Dylan, not bothering to turn round, which was a pretty stupid thing to do. Or at least that's what Martyn, our Photography tutor, said when he proceeded to give us a major, major bollocking. With, like, knobs on. No pun intended.

Martyn frogmarched me to my personal tutor who sent me home for the rest of the afternoon. Which actually is my kind of punishment.

As I stood outside the college gates applying some Vaseline to my lips, which seem to be permanently desensitised from over-use these days, Dylan caught up with me.

'Soooo, are we going back to yours?' he purred.

'No! I was *this* close to being sent home with a note,' I snapped. 'You know my parents don't trust us to be alone.'

It's true. They don't seem overjoyed about me dating Dylan and he's forbidden from my room unless the door's open. It hasn't occurred to them that we could get up to all sorts of inappropriate touching in plenty of other venues but I'm not going to be the one to shatter their illusions.

'Oh, c'mon Edie,' he said, nudging me. 'I don't want to go home and Martyn told me to get out of his sight for the rest of the day.'

'Well, OK, then,' I conceded. 'I need to talk to you anyway.'

'That sounds ominous,' Dylan said out of the side of

his mouth but then we spent the rest of the walk to my house in silence, which hacked me off.

It was like Dylan had forgotten how to speak to me.

'What the hell is your problem?' I blurted out the minute we got through the front door. 'Why aren't you talking to me?'

'I am,' he protested, following me up the stairs. 'You're the one who's not talking to me.'

'You're treating me like a . . . a . . . a kiss slut!' I said furiously.

Dylan snorted. 'Like, you don't treat me that way too.'

Then he sat down next to me on the bed and put an arm round my shoulders. 'Look, Eeds, this is a bit weird for both of us. So, what do you want to talk about then?'

I shrugged. 'Stuff. Like, y'know, stuff about each other. You never tell me what's going on with you.'

'The only thing going on with me is you,' Dylan snarked. 'There's nothing else to tell you about.'

If there was nothing else to talk about there was only one thing else to do: investigate each other's mouths with our tongues.

Two minutes later we were rolling about on my bed. I think it was when we landed on the floor with a loud thud that my mum realised that the house wasn't empty. She came charging up the stairs and banished

Dylan from the house forever for daring to lay his evil boy hands on her innocent, virginal daughter. It was all I could do to stop her from grounding me.

10th April

I didn't speak to Dylan today. I think the credit has run out on his phone. Which led to the revelation that I didn't have Dylan's home number. He always, always calls me. And that's weird. It's very weird. It's a whole world of weird. I've known Dylan for more than six months now. Been on intimate terms with his mouth for a little less time than that so you'd think I'd have his home phone number. I could have done the whole telephone directory thing but instead I went round to Shona's.

'So, are you going to have a go at me for not telling you about Dylan's dysfunctional family?' she wanted to know, a tad belligerently, when I asked her for his number.

I was like, woah!, but reined it back in. 'Look, I wouldn't expect you to betray Dylan's confidence,' I said sweetly. 'You're his oldest mate.' Which was actually her cue to explain what the hell she meant by her strange and cryptic remark about Dylan's family. His surname was strange, Kowalski (I think it's Polish or Czech or even Ukrainian or something), and I allowed myself a small daydream that Dylan's parents were dissidents from the former Eastern bloc and had come over to

England to start a new life with their little baby Dylan away from the harsh totalitarian regime and the jackboot of Communist oppression, but I think that was heavily influenced by the module I was studying in History.

I came back from a vision of Dylan's very young, very beautiful mother shielding a baby Dylan from a granite-faced Communist soldier to find Shona looking at me with an exasperated expression on her face. 'Did you enjoy the little trip you just took with the fairies?'

'Dylan hasn't said anything about having a dysfunctional family,' I said grumpily. 'In fact, he hasn't even admitted to having a family. I was beginning to think he was manufactured in an art boy factory.'

Shona fiddled nervously with some of the piles of junk on top of her bedside cabinet. 'Sorry,' she muttered. 'Sometimes it's hard being stuck in the middle of you two.'

Then Shona started telling me about the eye-raising stuff (can I just say, ewwwww?) she was getting up to with Paul and how she reckoned Mia was behind these weird phone calls she was getting and I forgot about ringing Dylan.

By the time I got home, it was really late and The Mothership was fuming. So, like, what else is new? She and Dad were heading off to the grandparents in Brighton for a long weekend (thank the sweet baby Jesus) and they were convinced I had Dylan stashed down the road somewhere and was just waiting for them to leave so he could enter the house and violate me on their new IKEA rug. She said as much. When your mother doesn't want to have the sex talk with you any more but instead wants to talk to you about the possibility that you might have sex on her soft furnishings, it's a watershed moment in any girl's life. I know I'll remember it fondly for many years to come.

Anyway after much foot-stamping and gagging noises, which I've found work much better than rational debate, I managed to persuade them that I hadn't seen Dylan all day and they left. Then they came back to harangue me with instructions about the boiler and not forgetting to give Pudding her worming tablets. Then they left again. Time for some fish fingers and Mum's *Downton Abbey* box-set, I think.

10th April (later)

Oh God, Dylan's on his way round. I wasn't going to let him but when he heard that the 'rents were off the premises for forty-eight hours there was no stopping him. He didn't exactly ask if he could stay over but then it's 10.30 pm now . . .

Oh, hell, that's him at the door now . . .

11th April

Dylan was practically leaning on the doorbell but straightened up when I took the security chain off and peered out.

'It'll be just my luck if you actually turn out to be a serial killer,' was my cheery greeting.

'Hey you,' he murmured with a fairly half-hearted smile. 'I brought you something.'

Usually when Dylan gets me a present it's kiss-related (lip balm, chocolate 'to boost your energy levels', etc.). So I was worried that it was like, alcohol or condoms or something and he was going to try and seduce me.

But when Dylan shoved a carrier bag at me, inside was a vintage red T-shirt with the Tizer logo on it.

'Aw, I love it,' I squealed, giving him a hug. I *did* love it and I was also really relieved that it wasn't going to lead to a BIG TALK ABOUT SEX.

'Try it on now!' Dylan insisted.

'You coming in? You can't stand on the doorstep all night.'

Him being there felt awkward all of a sudden – normally Dylan and I camp out in my bedroom but with the 'rents away it seemed wrong (which actually goes to show that all those Mother-sponsored talks about the dangers of teen pregnancy and having sex before I was ready did the trick).

But then again, I didn't want Dylan in the lounge with all my embarrassing school photos. I never noticed how small our hall was or what naff pictures we had until Dylan stood there looming over me and smirking at the reproduction Canalettos.

'Nice art,' he remarked. 'You can never have too many paintings of Venice in the late seventeenth century, I always say.'

'My parents went there on honeymoon,' I volunteered reluctantly. 'Where did your parents go?'

Words were coming out of my mouth. Really stupid words. I so needed to work on that.

Dylan ignored my crass attempt to ferret out any information that might have to do with his personal life.

'So, here we are,' he purred. 'And no authority figures within 200 miles.'

'Um, tea?'

Dylan followed me into the kitchen and watched through narrowed eyes as I put the kettle on and pondered the mug situation. Why did all our cups have slogans on them like, 'World's Best Dad' and 'Cat owner and proud of it'? I lived in the tackiest house in the world.

'Why are you acting like you're scared to be alone with me?' Dylan suddenly asked.

I blushed big time. 'I'm not.'

'I won't pounce on you just 'cause your parents are off the premises. Not unless you ask really nicely, that is.'

'God, don't be so cheesy,' I muttered. 'It just feels odd, that's all.'

By the time Dylan'd finished his tea it was past

midnight. I could tell that something was bothering him 'cause he hadn't tried to kiss me once. But as I walked past him to put his cup in the dishwasher, he pulled me onto his lap and buried his face in my neck.

I put my arms around him. 'I know there's something wrong, Dylan,' I said cajolingly. 'C'mon, tell me what's up.'

Dylan hugged me tighter. 'Oh, well . . . no, it's nothing.'

'Dylan!'

'My mum's chucked me out,' he finally said after I'd watched the second hand on the clock do a full 360 degrees. 'It's not serious, she does it a couple of times a month.'

'But why?' I gasped.

Dylan's lips twisted wryly. 'Nothing earth-shattering. I forgot to put the milk back in the fridge, and the time before that I came home a bit late. She's a bit irrational sometimes.'

I was completely out of my depth. When my mum's being irrational, it's usually because I've pinched her favourite earrings or changed all her email settings on the computer. And she would never, ever throw me out of the house. Ever.

'Maybe she's going through the menopause,' I suggested feebly and Dylan snorted. 'I'm sorry, D. I don't know what to say, just y'know, I'm sorry.'

I gently disentangled myself from his arms, so I could be the one that did the hugging. 'It will work itself out,' I told him because it seemed like the right thing to say.

Despite it being in actual fact a lame thing to say, Dylan seemed ridiculously pleased to be the huggee, rather than the hugger. 'Don't know what I'd do without you,' he mumbled into my hair.

And he totally slept in the spare room last night. Cross my heart and hope to die.

12th April

So the next day, Dylan got up and I gave him a clean towel so he could have a shower, then I made him breakfast before he went off to his Saturday job.

It was like we were living together or something.

We hadn't talked about whether he was going to come over later, or, like, stay the night again and I tried to spend the day working on a History essay that was due, but I mostly debated whether I should ring him and let him know that it was OK if he wanted to.

We usually hung out on a Saturday night anyway but I didn't want to seem like the pushy girlfriend. All the angsting had been for nothing though 'cause he rang and wanted to know if I fancied a bottle of wine with our dinner. So then I spent the rest of the afternoon fantasising that we *were* living together.

But it was in a cool Sex-and-the-City-style New York apartment and not a semi-detached house in Didsbury.

God, we had such a nice evening. I'd removed all traces of potentially humiliating family artefacts from the living room and we curled up on the sofa, sipping wine and talking nonsense.

We'd just had a lazy debate about whether Simon Cowell was the Antichrist when Dylan said out of the blue, 'You're lucky, you know. You have a nice house and you have two parents who take an active interest in your life . . . '

'You've got to be kidding me,' I spluttered before I'd had a chance to remove my foot from my mouth. 'My parents drive me absolutely crazy.'

'At least they're not, like, *actually* crazy,' Dylan said bitterly and the atmosphere in the room suddenly dropped to well below zero.

'I'm sorry. There's this whole thinking-before-I-say-stuff thing I'm trying out,' I groaned. 'It's not going very well.'

I hoisted myself to an upright position and placed my wine glass on the floor so I could swivel round and grab Dylan's hands. God, he looked so utterly miserable.

'You are lucky,' he said again. 'Your mum and dad . . . like, you're the most important person in their world. And even when you argue with them, it's about stuff that doesn't matter and they still love you. They'll never stop loving you.'

So then I felt really stupid and immature 'cause I'm always bitching about my parents and how they treat me like a little kid. And really, compared to Dylan who's currently homeless, I was just a spoilt little princess.

'I'm meant to argue with my parents,' I said in a small, lame voice. 'I'm a seventeen-year-old girl, it's my job.'

He smiled faintly at that and I leaned back on the cushions. We didn't say anything for a while and then Dylan stretched out across the sofa and put his head in my lap so I could wind my fingers through his hair. I swear to God, he almost purred. And when I rubbed his neck, which Pudding loves and which makes her legs do a good impersonation of spaghetti, he made happy, snuffly noises.

What with him being all boneless and relaxed, it seemed like as good a time as any. 'Dylan, I don't know much about you . . .'

Shit! Dylan tensed up immediately. For a moment I didn't think he was going to speak and then he was pouring out all this stuff about how his dad had walked out ten years ago and how he wanted to leave home but his mum was really unstable. How she'd pick fights with Dylan and say terrible things to him but then she'd have these hysterical tantrums every time he packed his bags. It was obvious he was really cut up about it 'cause once he'd started talking he couldn't stop. He kept wiping the back of his hand across his face, like he was trying not to cry and all I could do was carry on stroking his hair.

'Y'know, I guess I love her 'cause she's my mother,' Dylan said finally. 'But a large part of me sort of hates her.'

He hauled himself off the couch and stood up. 'I need some water, OK?'

When Dylan came back, he seemed much calmer but do you know what really pissed me off? He started making all these noises about how he should go and he didn't want to impose on me, but it was really because he'd opened up and he was totally embarrassed. I know him now. I don't automatically think he's, like, the coolest person in the world. Sometimes he's just an ordinary boy with severe emotional problems.

'Look, you can stay here tonight,' I protested. 'It's no big deal. Besides, you're already here and it's wicked late.'

Dylan stuck his hands into his back pockets and actually *pouted*! 'I usually go and camp at Simon's or Paul's or Shona's.'

That annoyed me. 'I can't believe you've never told me this,' I said sulkily.

OK, it wasn't what Dylan needed to hear but he'd confided in everyone except me.

Dylan flung himself back down on the sofa next to me and gave me a none-too-gentle poke in the ribs. 'Oh, don't start, Edie. I don't need you bitching at me too.'

I so wasn't going to stay in cuddling distance of him if he was going to be like that. But when I tried to get up, Dylan pulled me closer to him.

'Come here, you,' he drawled before kissing me hard. I pulled away.

'That's no way to end an argument,' I snapped.

'I thought we were just having a slight misunderstanding,' Dylan smirked. 'Anyway it's a nice way to end an argument.'

I pulled a face. Dylan was right. I hate it when that happens. (Not that it happens very often.)

We went up to my room to listen to the new Kate Nash album and it was just like Paris all over again. Dylan was going to sleep in the spare room but we began kissing and, well, I couldn't have moved even if I'd wanted to. Which I didn't.

13th April
Dylan woke up before me and tickled me until I started screaming.

'Do you have to be so damn perky?' I hissed, trying to untangle myself from my duvet. When you end up sleeping in your clothes, it always feels like you haven't really slept properly.

'Do you have to be so grumpy?' said Dylan teasingly. 'Your 'rents aren't coming back today, are they?'

'Not till Monday,' I grunted. 'Go 'way. I need more sleep.'

But I didn't get any more sleep 'cause Dylan got out of bed and put the telly on. And then provided me with a running commentary on how sucky all the bands were on MTV Hits until I finally gave up all pretence at having a lie-in and whined at him until he went to make some coffee.

It was very unsettling watching TV with Dylan. He watched me really intently every time someone naff was on screen and if I dared to blink, he'd snigger. 'You *so* fancy Jedward, don't you? Which one do you fancy more? Jed or Ward?'

It was a relief when both our phones rang at the exact same time. It was Shona on line one for me and Paul on line two for Dylan.

'I need to talk to you,' she cried. 'I'm coming round, OK?'

'But I'm still in bed . . .'

There was a ring on the doorbell. 'Too late Edie, I'm already here,' she announced before hanging up and banging on the door. She has no manners.

Dylan had finished speaking to Paul and he went to let her in. I thought they'd come up to my room but I could hear them talking in the hall while I got dressed.

Eventually I peered over the banister.

'What's happening?' I asked Shona, who was sitting on the stairs.

'It's Mia!' she spat out. 'She must have phoned fifty times last night. And I'm getting these pathetic letters. Look.'

She handed me a bunch of papers that said standard slasher-flick stuff like, 'I'm watching you,' 'Have you checked the locks?' and 'I'll see you if you ever get there.'

I rolled my eyes. 'Mia's really sad.'

'And not very imaginative,' said Dylan. 'D'you want me to have a word with her?'

'Cheers, hon,' beamed Shona, but there is *no* way I want Dylan to confront Mia. Not when they have a whole history that involves kissing and stuff.

NO WAY!

14th April

I begged Dylan not to get involved and to let Paul and Shona sort it out for themselves but he wasn't having it for a second.

'Shona doesn't want Paul anywhere near Mia, you know that,' he said in this long-suffering voice, like I'd been nagging. Which I *so* hadn't.

'Well, why can't she go and yell at Mia herself?' I wanted to know as we waited for the bus into town. 'She doesn't normally have a problem with that.'

Dylan sighed hard enough to blow the leaves off the

trees. 'She doesn't want Mia to know that she's getting to her and she's worried that she'll end up losing it and pushing her into the path of a tram or something.' His voice was all 'don't go there', but I still went there.

'But I don't see why you have to be the one who deals with it. You're not exactly a disinterested third party, are you?' My voice was rapidly reaching the shrill setting. 'Do you still fancy her?'

'No. Though when you start shouting like that, I'm not convinced that I still fancy you,' Dylan snapped.

And then I was so mad at him, I refused to get on the bus when it came. I just sat at the stop and in the end, Dylan crouched down in front of me and apologised profusely and said that he was sorry.

But, it was too late, he'd said it, and apologising didn't automatically wipe it out.

27th April

It's been, like, nearly two weeks and Dylan still hasn't sorted out the Mia business. The longer he leaves it, the more freaked out I get. And every time I mention it, Dylan gets really narked. Probably because I mention it a lot. Really a lot.

Like, yesterday, we were in the newsy's and I saw a coverline on a magazine that said something about exes and I couldn't stop myself. 'This Mia thing is a really bad idea, Dylan,' just kinda popped out of my mouth. 'I think you should leave it.'

Dylan looked to the heavens. 'Oh God, here we go again,' he muttered under his breath. 'Why don't *you* leave it instead?'

He was really snappy too.

2nd May

I feel so helpless, like Dylan's slipping through my fingers. This Mia thing is driving a wedge between us. Maybe I am being paranoid (Dylan told me I was last night) but I've always thought that there was unfinished business between Mia and Dylan.

The worst thing is that I can't even talk to Shona about it because she just doesn't *get* it.

'But why can't you and Paul sort it out yourselves?' I asked her as we walked around Vintage Dresses 'R' Us.

Shona shot me a withering look. 'Because I don't want her and him anywhere near each other. And if I went anywhere near her I'd end up thumping her,' she hissed at me. 'That girl's evil.'

'But it's all right for Dylan to be with her,' I mumbled. 'Even though they have a history.'

'You just have to trust him,' insisted Shona, conveniently forgetting that it was because she didn't trust Paul that Dylan got involved. 'He's meeting her tomorrow and then it will all be sorted. That reminds me! I had to get my mobile number changed so she'd stop sending me satanic text messages.'

And I was like, *tomorrow*! I started stressing about why Dylan hadn't told me. When I met him on his lunch-break, the atmosphere between us was icky with added bits of ickiness.

I couldn't help sulking while Dylan sat opposite me in Costa Coffee and stared resentfully at me from under his lashes.

We sat like that for another five minutes until Dylan suddenly stood up and snarled, 'And you wonder why I didn't tell you!' and stormed out.

3rd May

Today has been the worst day of my life, ever.

I'd gone out to lunch with the parents, even though it's about the most embarrassing thing in the world, and afterwards they'd decided to wander round furniture shops. Like, how boring. We were just synchronising watches so I could mooch elsewhere when out of the corner of my eye I saw Dylan striding purposefully towards St Anne's Square. I know I shouldn't have but I watched Dylan as he sat on a bench. And I watched as Mia walked up to him and kissed him on the cheek. And I watched as they walked off together and he put a hand under her elbow as they crossed the road and walked towards a café. I was just debating what to do next (reach into my ribcage and pull out my heart or spy on them some more) when I bumped into Nat and Trent – *literally*.

'What are *you* up to?' Nat asked.

'I'm not up to anything!' I said too quickly.

'Why don't I believe you?' laughed Trent but something in my face must have given the game away because they stopped teasing me and asked, in a dead concerned way, if I wanted to hang with them.

'I've got something I need to do,' I said, shaking my head. 'I'll see you tomorrow.'

I could tell that Nat in particular was desperate to know why I was acting like I had two weeks to live but he contented himself with sighing theatrically before he and Trent sauntered off.

I continued towards the café as if I had an invisible thread attached to me. As I got closer, I could see Mia and Dylan sitting next to each other at a window table. They were deep in conversation; he had his hand on her arm and she was ripping a tissue into tiny little pieces. She looked all kinds of deranged, in fact. Especially when she started to cry. I knew that Dylan wouldn't fall for it – whenever I threaten to turn on the waterworks, he just laughs and tells me not to be so predictable.

But when she began to sob, I reckoned that she was down to her last life and she hoped the tears would soften Dylan. I really did. In fact, I was just about to force myself to walk away when I saw Dylan pull Mia into his arms and then she was reaching up to kiss him.

Everything went black for a second and I thought I

was going to pass out. I could barely breathe. I shut my eyes and opened them again and hoped it was just a mirage but they were still kissing, his hands cupping her face. I know exactly how it feels to have his fingers resting against your cheek. It can really make a girl come undone. I dropped my bag because my fingers had suddenly lost their ability to grip and everything spilled out of it. As I stared at the make-up and the pens and the coins scattered on the ground, I couldn't summon the energy to bend down and pick them up. I just wanted to get the hell out of there. As I staggered away, Dylan looked up and saw me.

Too late. Too late. It was all too late.

3rd May (but later)

Oh God, how could I have been so stupid? I'm like, Queen of the Losers. We were doomed from the start. Like, I was always more into Dylan than he was into me. And I'd practically forced him into being my boyfriend. It wasn't like he ever wanted to go out with me. And I knew I should be angry at them, at Dylan and Mia, but I should have known I wouldn't be able to keep him.

And when I got in after just walking and walking, Mum was yelling because I hadn't been at the allotted meeting place and they couldn't ring me because I'd left my mobile on the freakin' pavement. I walked up the stairs and then she was yelling at me again because

Dylan was on the phone and even though I didn't want to speak to him I picked up the receiver to hear Dylan say in that throaty way of his, 'We need to talk,' and all the stuff inside of me collapsed. 'I'll see you tomorrow on the bridge,' he added, while the tears spilled down my face.

4th May

I wore black to match my mood. As I shrugged myself into slouchy trews and a shirt, all I could think about was that I didn't have anything to say to him. There was nothing to say. It was impossible to make it all right. Things were messed and there was no way to unmess them.

To be honest, I s'pose I half-hoped that Dylan would tell me everything was going to be OK and I'd got it all wrong. But they'd been kissing. You can't come back from a kiss you gave to someone else when your girlfriend had got a ringside seat.

It was one of those perfect days. The sky was that sort of blue you always want to paint your bedroom walls but you can never find the right colour on the paint charts. I wished it was raining.

Dylan was wearing jeans and the cool Hawaiian shirt we'd found at a Crimbo jumble sale. I watched him standing on the bridge for a minute and even after all this time just looking at him could make my stomach dip; he still had the power to make me feel all unnecessary. That was half the problem. The sun was glinting off his hair and as he saw me he straightened up and put a hand to his eyes to shield them from the glare. Or maybe he couldn't bear to look at me 'cause as he walked towards me I knew I had a really accusing look on my face.

I sat down on the bench under the willow tree.

'Hey you,' Dylan said, as he sat down next to me.

'Hey,' I muttered quietly. I looked at my toes poking out of my flip-flops like they were really fascinating. Dylan shifted restlessly next to me.

'So is this the silent treatment?' he asked. 'You not talking to me?'

All I could think about was him kissing Mia.

'I'm not *not* talking to you,' I mumbled. 'I *can't* talk to you.'

'Well that's helpful.'

Dylan was meant to be full of apologies and excuses and promises that it would never, ever happen again. He wasn't meant to be so bloody difficult.

'I should have known that something like this was going to happen,' I said in a rush. Dylan turned to look at me with a guarded expression on his face. 'I mean, you don't tell me anything. Like, you wouldn't have told me about your mum if she hadn't chucked you out. And you didn't even tell me that you were going to see Mia yesterday until I found out from Shona.'

Dylan rolled his eyes. 'That's because you've been

going on about it for weeks. It's, like, all you could talk about,' he spat out. 'OK, so what do you want to know about my oh-so-fascinating life? C'mon, I'll tell you anything.'

But there was nothing left that I really needed to know. I'd seen him kiss Mia. And that was it. There was a pause before I said: 'This just isn't working, is it?'

'What? This conversation or us?' Dylan asked like he didn't really want me to tell him.

'Us,' I said in a tiny voice. 'I think we should stop seeing each other.' I'm sure I only said it because I wanted Dylan to tell me that he was going to make everything better but he didn't. He gave me such a venomous look that I could feel myself shrinking back against the bench to try and get away from it.

'You know, Edie, that's fine by me,' he finally drawled. 'I thought you were different but you're just a lightweight. You can't cope with anything that exists outside of the dream world you live in.' He stood up and walked off without even looking at me. All I could think as I made my way home was that he'd never even told me that he loved me.

5th May

I feel terrible. Really terrible. I didn't think having a broken heart would make me feel so achey and nauseous and sore-throaty. I just want to die.

17th May

Do you know what works really well when you're trying to avoid bastard, jerkface ex-boyfriends? Going down with gastric flu, that's what.

I've missed the last couple of weeks of college due to puking my guts up and being generally delirious. Mum even took time off work, that's how ill I've been. But it was kinda nice. She parked me on the sofa with a quilt around me and we watched old black-and-white movies on TCM and when I wasn't crying or throwing up, she'd stroke my hair.

Dylan is maintaining radio silence. Shona came round once when I was sleeping and she must have told him I was ill but I didn't get so much as a Get Well Soon card from him. Because he cares *that* much.

Today I felt better. I ate scrambled eggs and actually managed to keep them down, which is so of the good. Because I've lost, like, a stone and my tits, which weren't exactly filling out a B-cup anyway, have shrunk to little bee stings. Then I realised that Dylan would be leaving college in about a month and going off to someplace else to do his degree in September. And I'm trying really hard to hate him but just the thought of him not being *here* made me cry all over again. You'd have thought my tear ducts would have dried up by now.

21st May

I'm recovered and trying to catch up on all the college

work I've missed. I'm only crying about every other hour now and I was even allowed out to meet Shona for a coffee.

It was a little awkward. We made polite small talk about a band who were playing soon and tried not to mention the D word until I burst into tears. Again.

'Oh Edie,' she murmured sympathetically. 'You've really screwed up this time and you look awful.'

'*I've* screwed up?!' I spluttered. '*I* didn't go and snog someone else.'

'Dylan didn't . . .' she started. 'Look, you two need to talk.'

I shook my head violently and wiped a hand across my eyes. 'That's just it, we can't. We were dreadful together. We were, like, the worst couple ever. All we did was argue and get off with each other; it's not exactly the basis for a relationship, is it?'

Shona squeezed my hand. 'I could speak to him.'

I pulled a face. 'What's the point? He doesn't care. I didn't see him bringing flowers and bunches of grapes over when I was sicking my guts up. He didn't think we were worth fighting for.'

'Well, neither did you.'

'Gee, thanks, Shona, now turn the knife counter-clockwise,' I snapped, but I couldn't help myself. 'Has he said anything about me?'

'I haven't seen that much of him,' Shona insisted. 'He's shut himself away. Look, why don't you come and see Bikini Dust next week? Just you and me. We'll have a girls' night out.'

'I guess.' I sighed. 'At least it'll get Mum off my back.'

'Well, that's settled then,' said Shona with a triumphant gleam in her eyes.

27th May

I didn't fancy going to see Bikini Dust play. I wanted to skulk around my room and listen to my completely depressing mope-rock playlists that I've been making but Shona forced me out of the house. It was my first big outing since I got ill and I looked utterly revolting; all scrawny and pasty so it probably wasn't a good idea to wear black. I looked like a total Goth. Worse, I looked like a Goth with a smack habit.

Shona was acting all twitchy and weird too. I asked her when the band was coming on about five times before I actually managed to get a reply. And no wonder. Because we'd only been there ten minutes when Dylan strolled in. I hadn't seen him for nearly a month and I figured I'd managed to wean myself off him. He had on this disgusting pair of checked wool trousers that Shona and I had begged him to never wear in public and a bizarre pale blue shirt with ruffles down the front. But who was I kidding? He'd never seemed more beautiful or more out of my reach. Though he really needed a haircut, I could hardly look at his face, at his cheekbones and the glitter of his eyes so I kept my gaze firmly on his black Chuck Taylors.

'You didn't tell me *he* was going to be here?' I yelped at Shona before hurrying off when I saw him striding over in our direction. I hid behind a speaker stack and watched Dylan having a go at Shona, judging from the expressions on both their faces.

It wasn't until the band came on that Dylan suddenly appeared beside me.

His eyes were boring into me but I refused to acknowledge him until he bent down slightly and hissed in my ear: 'So are you better now?'

'I'm fine.'

'You don't look fine. You look like the poster girl for flu,' was his charming reply.

'Ta, ever so,' I muttered but I don't think he heard.

'I got into the Fine Art course at the university so I'm staying in Manchester,' he continued. Although I would never have admitted it to anyone I felt a tide of relief wash over me. But I just said, 'Whatever.'

'It's nice to find you in such a talkative mood, Eeds.'

I turned round to face him. 'What the hell do you expect?' I screeched. 'I'm meant to be all happy and pleased to see you? After all the crap you've put me through?'

Dylan grabbed my shoulders and hauled me against him. 'So what do you think happened, Edie?' he shouted at me.

'I saw Mia with her tongue down your throat!' I screamed, suddenly realising that it was the quiet bit between songs and most of the audience were staring at us.

The band started up again as Dylan bit out: 'Yeah, you saw Mia kissing *me.*' He shook me gently. 'But you didn't wait round for explanations.'

'You've had three weeks to think up an excuse.' I slapped his hands off me. 'And it's not even a good one.'

'I shouldn't need to make up excuses, you should trust me!'

'So you admit it was an excuse?' I pounced.

Dylan shot me a look of complete disgust. 'You can't even see what's right in front of you! Just grow up, sweetheart!' He pushed me away but I grabbed his arm and started yelling about what a pig he was. He yelled right back that I was immature and needy. We were making so much noise that the lead singer of Bikini Dust halted the song and told us to shut up.

I've never been so mortified in my whole life – Dylan and I were *escorted* off the premises by two bouncers. Of course, then I started crying (which is getting to be a really old look for me) and Dylan started being nice to me, which involved hugging and hair-stroking and we ended up having this intense kissing session. Dylan had me backed up against the wall of the club when Shona, Nat and Trent burst through the door.

'You two sort it out for God's sake!' Shona barked at

us before disappearing. Dylan went rushing after her. And me? I went home.

3rd June

I did something either really stupid or incredibly brave today, depending on your politics. I went and spoke to Mia.

It took me ages to find her but eventually I tracked her down to the library basement, where you can smoke without setting off any alarms.

Normally Mia's the definition of brazen but she seemed quite taken aback when she saw me padding towards her through the stacks.

'You look like shit,' she said, but it lacked the usual bite.

'I need to talk to you about Dylan,' I said, sticking to what I rehearsed. 'I saw you kissing a few weeks ago and I want to know what's going on.'

She nibbled on a fingernail while I folded my arms and waited for a response. 'Have you asked him?' she said eventually.

I shrugged. 'He said *you* were kissing *him*. Didn't look like that to me.'

She gave me one of those cat-like smiles of hers that make me want to punch her. And she had on this completely ridiculous T-shirt that she'd slashed so it would look punk but really I think she just wanted people to look at her tits.

'Me and Dylan go way back,' she said. But see, normally with Mia she spurts out all this evil crap right off the bat and this time she wasn't. She was actually taking time to engage her brain cells before she opened her mouth.

'I know but I'm not talking about way back, I'm talking about a few weeks ago.' I was being so calm. I couldn't begin to imagine why. 'You know we've split up?'

Mia's head shot up from where it had been contemplating the end of her cigarette. 'Because of me?'

'Well, yeah . . .' I perched on the edge of the table. 'It's kinda hard to carry on seeing someone once they've kissed their ex-girlfriend.'

'Oh, but I was never his ex-anything,' Mia protested. 'It was just to make Paul jealous . . .'

And then she did something that I never expected her to do in front of me. She burst into tears.

It wasn't to make me feel sorry for her, it was proper crying. With snot and howling and her hands over her eyes. I found a tissue in the bottom of my bag *and then I put my arms around her*!

'Paul . . . love him . . . can't bear it,' was about all the sense I managed to get out of her for a while.

But finally she stopped crying and was at the stage where you scrub at your face with a ratty tissue and hiccup gently. 'I know you think I'm the biggest bitch in the world,' she spluttered. 'But I love Paul, I really love him and I can't stand to see him with *her* and he's happy and it's not because of me.'

'Oh Mia,' I said sadly, 'I'm sorry but you and Paul, it was so messed to begin with, it couldn't have lasted.'

Well that set her off again and my shoulder was soggy with her tears. 'The thing with the letters, I was just being a crazy person. And then Dylan wanted to meet and I thought he was going to yell at me but he was so nice about it. You know? When he's being sweet and understanding?'

I nodded and tried to swallow the planet-sized lump that had suddenly lodged itself in my throat.

'And it wasn't a "get it on" kiss, I just felt so lonely and he was there and it was a . . . a . . . *friendly* kiss and it was my idea, not his. I swear, Edie! You and me, we're not mates, but I never thought you and Dylan would break up over this. I thought you'd have sorted it out.'

But we hadn't. And we couldn't. So I started crying and getting snot on Mia's shoulder. Then she started crying again. It was a regular weepfest.

Sometimes people that you barely know, barely even like, are the ones that get you. And for ten minutes me and Mia were soulmates. She was angsting about Paul and my heart had broken over Dylan and we were entirely on the same abandoned girlfriend wavelength.

'So what are you and Dylan going to do?' she asked me half an hour later, as we walked along the canal path with a Mr Whippy apiece.

'I don't know,' I admitted. 'Things had been not so good before the kiss and just bloody awful after that.'

'But you love him, right?'

Oh God. The tears were threatening a rematch. 'I love him but he doesn't love me. On a good day, he might want to shag me if I was willing and that's about it. And if you tell anyone that, I promise that I will kill you.'

When we parted in town, there was no point in saying that we'd meet up for trips to the cinema and stuff. We weren't friends. But I don't think Mia and I are enemies any more. And that's actually kinda cool.

8th June

I miss Dylan.

10th June

Maybe if I told Dylan that I know what really happened with him and Mia we could get back to how we were. But he should have told me. Made the effort to make me understand, instead of getting all defensive and cold-shouldery. He said that I should trust him but shouldn't he have trusted me with the truth? Plus, would it have freaking killed him to send me a Get Well Soon card?

17th June

So, Dylan and I live in the same town, we go to the same college and today is the first time I've seen him in twenty-one days. Because he's so very obviously avoiding me. I haven't been going to Photography because I've had so much work to catch up on, but Martyn put a note in my pigeonhole which said that there was no pressure but it'd be nice to see me before the end of the year.

I knew Dylan would be there, which is why I spent, like, twenty minutes putting on make-up before the class. Which is just sad and stupid especially as the effect I was going for was the natural look.

Anyway I got there late because I always get everywhere late and I sat at the back in my usual spot, right next to Dylan, Simon and Paul. When I walked in, Dylan looked up and nodded at me, then turned back to listen to Martyn.

It hurt that he did that. Like I was just some casual acquaintance instead of someone who he cared for. The night he stayed over when my parents were in Brighton, I'd woken up at one point and his hand had been resting right over my heart. Like the thump thump thump had reassured him. We'd had real intimacy and now all I got was a nod.

At the end of the class, it just became worse. As I got up to leave, I brushed past him and he turned to look at me. 'You all right then?' he asked.

'I'm fine,' I said and I walked out.

30th June

You know, I don't think I want to keep a diary any more. What's the point? I read back what I've written in here and it just makes it hurt all over again.

I don't really like who I am at the moment, I don't see Shona because she's Dylan's friend and I know I won't be able to hang out with her and not want to know how he is. And I scuttle straight home these days, I don't go to Fritzsch's and I don't go clubbing because I just can't bear to see him. He always says hi and it's worse than him not talking to me at all.

7th July

To: artboy@hotmail.com
From: cutiesnowgirl@hotmail.com

Hey Dylan

I just thought I'd let you know that I'm going to be spending the next couple of months in Brighton at my grandparents. I think my mum and dad are still in a state of shock that I want to spend the summer so sedately.

I just need to sort myself out a bit.

I spoke to Mia a little while ago and she told me what happened that day. I kinda wish that maybe you could have told me instead but you didn't. Maybe it was better that we split up, we seemed to fight a lot, didn't we? And I always got the feeling that you thought I was immature. Like, I acted too young or something.

For what it's worth, I've done a lot of thinking and you are right. I didn't trust you enough but it's hard to trust someone who doesn't want to let you into his life. I don't really know where I'm going with this. I'm sorry that it didn't work out between us and I wanted you to know that.

I think about you a lot and I do miss you. I feel like I've changed a lot since it all went wrong and now I can see that I should never have forced you to go out with me. I hope we can still be friends. When I get back from Brighton in September, maybe we can go to the cinema or something?

Anyway, just wanted to clear the air between us.

Have a good summer and take care,

Edie

10th September

I'm back in Manchester and I've decided to keep a diary again. It was either that or walk around talking to myself all day. So summer was good, much better than I expected. The edited highlights:

- I gained all the weight I lost from being ill due to my grandmother stuffing me full of home-cooked food all day. Like I was a pig going to market.
- I caught up with all my old friends and that was good. It wasn't as good as it used to be but we had a laugh.
- I read every single Jane Austen novel.
- I went to Cornwall for a week to stay with the other grandparents and went to a rave on the beach. I had a bit of a holiday romance with this surfer boy called Marcus. He tried to teach me how to surf; I didn't get it. I tried to teach him about Jane Austen; he didn't get it. But the kissing was OK. It wasn't even a tenth as good as certain kisses I've had but I figure it's like falling off a horse. You have to get straight back on.
- I had highlights put in my hair so now it is truly blonde.
- And one last thing – I got my groove back. I can't believe how I became this total misery chick before I went to Brighton. Well, I'm just so over all of that. I'm over *him*.

13th September

I went clubbing with Nat and Trent and was just coming out of the loo when I spotted Dylan. I'd forgotten how he could make me feel just by looking at me with that half-smile of his. Except I was totally over him now and his art-boy charms no longer worked on me. As I walked calmly over to him, I certainly wasn't thinking about how I wanted his arms around me. Not one little bit.

'Hey you,' I said to him, smiling because I didn't have a care in the world.

Dylan didn't look unpleased to see me but then he didn't exactly look like all his birthdays had come at once. 'Oh hey,' he replied, tugging at the collar of his shirt. 'So you're back?'

'Looks like it, doesn't it?' I tossed my newly-blonder hair over my shoulder and raised my eyebrows at him. 'So how have you been?'

I was so busy trying to appear cool and yet ultimately unavailable that it seemed like a really good idea not to make eye contact with Dylan. Over the summer I'd turned him into a shorter, scrawnier, sloppily dressed version of the real thing. And now standing by the cigarette machine with the actual tall, lean and, OK, still sloppily dressed real thing was unsettling. Had his eyes always been that piercing? Or his bottom lip so full that I wanted to take it between my teeth and bite it?

I was so intent on trying not to stare at Dylan that when he took hold of my hands, I gave a start. 'I missed you,' he was saying. 'I wanted to get in touch with you but then stuff came up.'

My stupid, foolish heart, which was always going

to get me into trouble, stopped beating for a second. 'What kind of stuff?'

'Who's this?' said a voice behind me. I turned round to see this beautiful girl with long red hair standing, glaring at me. She sidled up to Dylan and wrapped an arm round his waist before repeating herself. 'Who the hell is this, Dylan?'

14th September

What kind of stupid name is Veronique anyway? No-one's called Veronique! No-one except Dylan's *new girlfriend*! Yeah, that's how much he was missing me! He was so busy pining over me that he managed to cop off with some stupid posh girl from Cheshire. I mean, whatever.

And she *so* dyes her hair.

I even tried talking to Mum today. I was that desperate. She was all like, 'I know Dylan's very special to you but getting over your first serious boyfriend is always hard.' Thanks Mum, way to go.

17th September

Shona wasn't much more help. Apparently Dylan met 'Veronique' on this open day at the university and she's studying Performance Art but Shona was tight-lipped about anything else.

'I don't want to get involved Edie,' she said while we were meant to be watching the new Emma Stone film and getting tutted at for talking by this saddo man sitting behind us. 'I'm not taking sides.'

Paul was waiting outside the cinema. They were going to some party. I wasn't really into it but then Paul said, 'Look, Edie, I think Dylan and Veronique (her name just gets more and more pretentious every time I hear it!) are going. It could be awkward.'

I looked to Shona for support. She put an arm round my shoulders. 'You wouldn't make a scene, would you, hon?'

I shrugged her off furiously. 'Oh I see, it's all right for Dylan to be a two-timing git and break my heart and then go out with someone else without even having a decent break-up interval but if I get upset, it's all "Oh there's Edie being all hysterical",' I screamed hysterically. 'I don't want to go to the stupid party anyway.'

Then I stormed off in the opposite direction to the bus stop and had to walk home.

27th September

Nat is the only one who understands. While I was away Nat and Trent split up. Trent's off to university while Nat's staying behind and they had this big fight about whether long-distance relationships could work.

We spend all our time together watching weepy movies and eating ice cream. I'm allowed to rant on about Dylan as long as Nat can do the same about Trent. But he doesn't have any answers. Only questions along the lines of, 'Why are boys so insensitive?' and 'How come two fabulous people like us are on our own?'

He's like the Carrie Bradshaw of Manchester. Except gay and a boy.

1st October

Just when it couldn't get any worse Mum decided that I needed to get a part-time job. I hate it when she goes into one of her Edie efficiency drives. She's stopped my allowance! And even worse, she's got me an interview at the Sunshine Café next door to Rhythm Records where Dylan works.

I think sometimes she lies in bed at night and plots ways to make my life suck.

There can be no other explanation.

3rd October

I got the job! Anna, who owns the café, was very impressed with my tea-making abilities (it's all to do with how many times you dunk the tea bag). She's a little hippy woman who told me that she realised that serving up carrot cake was never going to make her rich and so she branched out into fry-ups. Actually she's nice and funny, though she should probably rethink the tie-dye leggings. They're so not a good look.

I'm going to work Saturdays and Wednesday and Thursday afternoons when I don't have college. Anna said it would be a good idea if I could smile a bit more but as long as I could wash up and carry two plates at once I was hired. I might as well get paid for it instead of doing it at home for free.

11th October
Dylan came into the café today. Even though I hate him I still love him too. I don't have the answers to that one.

He looked really sad when he saw me walking over. Probably because he couldn't believe that he used to date someone who was now employed as a skivvy.

'Hey Edie,' he said softly. 'I thought you'd disappeared off the face of the earth.'

It killed me but I managed to summon up a smile so wide it made my face ache. 'Nope, I'm still here. Are you ready to order?'

I could feel his eyes on me while I made coffees and recited the specials. When I went to clear his table, he'd left me a note saying 'Call me'. Yeah. I'll see him in hell first. And then later on in the afternoon, Dylan's mate Simon came in and I suddenly realised where I could find the answers.

We chatted while I took his order and then I asked him if he fancied going for a drink later. I've never actually asked a boy out before but it wasn't like I was asking Simon *out* out and he didn't seem to think there was anything weird about it.

I'd never really got to know Simon. He always seemed so . . . adult with his glamorous girlfriends and steady stream of sarcastic remarks. He's sort of intense and I'd always felt that he didn't approve of me and Dylan. Like he thought I was really shallow because I moaned about my parents and made Dylan take me to see films with cute boys in them.

Anyway we went to the pub and he ordered me a beer and I didn't want to seem uncool so I drank it and tried not to pull a face. We talked about Brighton and Simon's new job at a design company. We had a couple more beers and then I started asking my questions. But Simon wasn't biting.

'Look Edie,' he said brutally, tearing up his beermat with great vigour. 'You went running off at the first sign of trouble. Why should you care who he's seeing? You spent all your time giving Dylan grief so you can't blame him for bailing out.'

'But he kissed Mia,' I whimpered. It sounded really lame and about time I just let it go.

'Or she kissed him,' said Simon. 'Whatever. It was bloody months ago! Why are you still obsessing about it?'

'So is he serious about Veronique?' I asked, running a finger down the condensation on my pint glass.

Simon shrugged and tried to hide his amused smile. 'Ask him yourself, babes.'

'This is all a big joke to you,' I hissed at him. 'You think I'm some stupid little kid. Well, I'm not. You don't know how much I'm hurting.'

He had the nerve to actually laugh, like my hurt was really not that important in the grand scheme of things. 'You've had too much to drink. C'mon I'll take you home.'

I put a hand on his arm as he tried to stand up. 'Simon, please. I know you think I'm some silly little girl and I'm not cool or pretty . . .'

Simon gave my hand a squeeze and sat down again. 'I don't think that Edie,' he said quietly. 'Yeah, you're not what Dylan needs but I always thought you were cute. Very cute.'

I *had* had too much to drink 'cause next thing I'm whispering, 'Do you really think I'm cute?' and leaning forward so Simon could kiss me.

He did kiss me. Hard. With his hand cupping the back of my head so I couldn't get loose. And I didn't really want to. It was a really fantastic kiss but it wasn't the answer. Then we were both pulling away at the same time.

'That was a mistake . . .' we gasped in unison.

13th October

Nat and I went and sat on the wall by the Art block to

check out the new intake of Art Foundation students or 'the autumn collection' as he calls it. I'm strictly window-shopping and failing to see anyone who would bring out the blue in my eyes.

Dylan and Simon came into the café again and Dylan acted like everything was cool between us. I wondered if he'd ever speak to me again if he knew that I'd kissed Simon.

Then that stupid Veronique came in with Shona who hasn't returned my calls since I had that hissy fit at her outside the cinema. They were being like best friends or something while I had to *wait* on them! They could have the decency to find another place to hang out.

The whole thing made me feel really crappy. I used to be where Veronique was – with Dylan's arm round my shoulders and Shona laughing at my jokes. They didn't even leave a decent tip!

16th October

When I finished work today, Dylan was waiting for me outside. When I saw him slouched against the wall in his scuffed leather jacket and his black cords, I felt such a sharp pang of longing that it almost made me gasp.

I looked skanky. My hair was scraped back into a ponytail (albeit a very blonde ponytail); I was wearing my tattiest jeans and a holey cardigan.

'Hey you,' he murmured.

'Look, it's late, I'm tired, make it quick,' I muttered, not looking at him.

'Oh Eeds,' Dylan sighed. 'Can we just go for a drive and sort things out?'

I thought about it for precisely five seconds. 'I s'pose so.'

We ended up driving all the way to Blackpool. It's hard to explain but sitting next to Dylan in the tiny confines of his car and him *driving* me somewhere – it suddenly felt like we were cocooned away from the rest of the world. I thought we'd stay like that forever and just keep driving. Or maybe I just wished it. Neither of us really spoke but it would have killed the mood or the truce that we'd declared as soon as I let Dylan help me into the passenger seat.

In fact, we didn't say much until we were sat in a shelter on the prom, sharing a bag of chips and bracing ourselves against the stiff, salt-tinged breeze that swept in from the sea.

'C'mon then, talk,' I said once the chips had gone and my lips were sore from the wind and the sharp tang of the vinegar.

Dylan leant back on the seat and looked at me consideringly. 'So . . . Mia kissed me. Not the other way round but every time I thought about telling you, it just sounded lame. Like a really crap excuse. What else? Well, I started going out with Veronique because we were finished according to your email and . . . I'd do anything to be your friend, Edie. I miss you so much.'

I sat there, trying to take it all in. And I knew he was telling the truth about everything. It made what I had to say so much harder.

'I kissed Simon the other week after I'd had too much to drink,' I said very quietly and I wasn't sure he'd even heard me over the howl of the wind.

Then Dylan was hugging me tightly and I wrapped my arms around him and never wanted him to let me go. 'Is that why you've been avoiding me? Edie, I don't mind. I just want us to . . .'

'But I want you to mind!' I cried, fighting to get out of his embrace when only a second before I'd wanted to stay there forever. 'I want you to be angry 'cause then I'll know that you loved me.'

Dylan gently took hold of my chin. 'But I did love you.'

'You never once told me that.'

'I'll always love you Edie,' Dylan whispered right into my ear. 'But it wasn't working out. I made you unhappy, you made me unhappy and now we need to move on. So, please, let's just do the friend thing.'

I leant forward and kissed him really softly on the lips. Maybe there were a couple of tears trickling down my face but I could probably pass them off as my eyes watering due to the gusts rolling in across the waves.

'OK, friends then.' I sniffed. 'And what the hell is Shona's problem anyway?'

Dylan laughed and threw his arm round my shoulder so I could nestle against him to keep warm. Which is what he probably wanted me to think but I couldn't help but fixate on how he'd just said that he'd always love me. So, what he meant was that he did love me. He *loved* me. And he still loves me. Which is why I'm not buying this friends crap. He wouldn't be going out with Veronique if I hadn't written that stupid, confused email before I went to Brighton. And if he still loves me, it means that anything could happen. Which is why I agreed to meet him and his new university friends for drinks when he was driving me back home. Plus I really want to suss out Veronique.

28th October

I spent all day working on my 'I just threw this stuff on' look. I had my highlights re-done and got the hairdresser to put my hair up in this messy bun thing. I'd blown my entire week's wages on new Top Shop jeans and a 1940s black satin top from the really expensive vintage shop in town. I looked about as good as it's humanly possible for me to look but I was still shaking as I pushed open the door of the bar.

I spent several moments feeling like a complete prat

as I frantically searched around for Dylan before I saw him and his mates chilling out on some sofas.

Walking towards ten people who are staring at you is very off-putting. I kept my head up and tried not to bite my lip.

Then Shona jumped up and was hugging me, and Dylan was introducing me as 'the coolest girl I've ever known'.

Veronique looked unimpressed while this lanky boy with a quiff called Carter (Carter!) had the audacity to say, 'Edie? What kind of a weird name is that?'

I looked to Dylan for support but he was too busy kissing Veronique to notice. As evenings go, it wasn't too bad. If, like, your only other option was to have your eyes gouged out or something.

Turned out that Carter is actually Veronique's brother, which explains why a) he had a stupid name and b) he was so aggravating. He asked me if I called myself Edie because of Edie Sedgwick and when I pulled a face to suggest that I didn't know what the hell he was talking about he had the nerve to say, 'I'm sorry, I guess the 1960s New York underground scene is a little too sophisticated for your tastes.'

I would have worked up to a really crushing reply but I still didn't have any idea what he was banging on about, 'cept he was managing to make me look like an idiot in front of five people I didn't know. Shona shrugged apologetically and Paul started this long, complicated explanation to do with Andy Warhol, and Veronique and Dylan were *still* investigating each other's back molars.

I had one drink and then pretended that I had an elsewhere to be, which was actually home to my bed, where I curled up with Pudding who could tell that I was down and didn't try to claw me to pieces when I cried into her fur.

31st October
I've finally got a clue. I am not going anywhere near Dylan again. If he comes into the café, which he does with alarming regularity, I'm going to be polite but apart from that, I am avoiding him. As far as I'm concerned, he should have a 'Warning! Haz Chem!' label tattooed on his forehead. He's out of bounds as a friend, as someone who may or may not still be in love with me, as someone who is sucking face with another girl. He is out of my life, once and for all. I mean it, this time. I might not have meant it the other times, but I'm serious. No more Dylan.

1st November
I've been Dylan-free for forty-eight hours. It's going pretty well.

5th November
Still Dylan-free. He came into the café today but I got

Poppy, the other waitress, to serve him. And I managed not to make eye contact the whole time he was in there. I pretty much rock!

8th November
Still Dylan-free and thank God that I can screen his calls on my mobile. I wish he'd get the message to just leave me the fuck alone.

14th November
Turns out that Dylan doesn't just play games with my heart when I'm with him. Oh no. He can do it via the medium of email too.

To: cutiesnowgirl@hotmail.com
From: artboy@hotmail.com

Oh Edie, Edie, Edie

You seem to have fallen off the face of the earth. After our trip to Blackpool I thought we'd agreed to be friends but after one hanging-out session with my mates, you disappeared and left no clues.

Shona's being annoyingly unhelpful about the whole business. I think she feels guilty about having to side with me out of long-term loyalty when she'd rather side with you out of some kind of misguided sisterly solidarity. But she did put forward the theory that seeing Veronique and me together was like 'someone cutting out your heart without an anaesthetic'. But I don't get it. 'Cause sometimes, Edie, I think you're all heart and I worry about how you get hurt by everything from sad puppies on YouTube to reckless art boys who won't fall into line. And then there are the other times when you act like you don't have a heart at all. Maybe I shouldn't even go there. But there were so many times when you brushed me aside without even listening to what I had to say. Like, as if I'd ever want Mia again after I'd had you in my arms.

So, anyway I don't think it was seeing me and Veronique together that's caused your complete absence from my life. I did hear you having an angry exchange with Carter (when I heard you hissing at him it brought back memories of that awful argument we had in the dining room of the hideous Hôtel Du Lac) but I can't believe that one sardonic sculpture student with a love of stirring it up could send you scurrying into hibernation. (He thought you were a complete babe, by the way.)

The only explanation I can have for the way the girl I formerly knew as Edie is never in when I call or has always just gone on her lunch when I go to the café where she works (why do you take your lunch-break at 5pm anyway?) or has already made plans with Shona is that she hates me. Irrevocably hates me and there's no cure.

But I don't hate *you*, Edie. You bug the hell out of me but I still miss you like mad. Don't get me wrong, I'm really into Veronique but there'll always be a little part of me that's yours alone. I think you must have cast a spell on me. I miss the way you pull the caramel off a Twix and then nibble the chocolate round the edges before finally eating the rest of the bar in three decisive bites. I miss you reading books about crazy girls (they always reminded me of you) while I lay on your bed and looked up at the cloudy sky that you'd painted on your bedroom ceiling. And I miss the way you'd bite your lip and blush when you wanted me to kiss you. But, most of all, I miss those kisses and how right it felt to hold you.

Like I said when we went to Blackpool I'll always love you but I just can't be with you, Edie. When we were together I spent all my time walking on eggshells while you suspected me of chasing other girls. And those glimpses of that other Edie, the one who doesn't have a heart, became more and more frequent. I s'pose what really finished us off was the way you disappeared to Brighton for weeks after sending me that email, that was like an exercise in doublespeak. I needed a codebreaker just to understand what you were talking about and before I could even ask you, you'd gone. And for the record, I always thought it was *you* who chucked *me*.

Those weeks that you were in Brighton were some of the worst weeks of my life. I felt like you'd stolen half my soul away and then I met Veronique. I'm not just going out with her on the rebound, I really like her. She gets me. I get her. There's no confusion. And I think the two of you would really get on if you gave each other a chance. But I guess that's the last thing you want to hear. What I'm really writing to tell you is that I'm finally moving out of my mum's house (I can't take the stress any more) and getting a flat with Simon, Carter and Paul. All the details are at the bottom of this email so you know where to find me.

I guess you still think that I treated you terribly and that I was only interested in getting you into bed (which is only slightly true) but I'll tell you one thing, ten years from now when you're doing fabulous things and making the world weep with wonder, I'm going to come and find you so we can go on that road trip we always talked about and raise a family of beautiful, artistically precocious little freaks.

Come back wherever you are.

Toxically yours

Dylan

Why does he always do this? Just when I want him to let me go, he always finds a way to come hurtling back into my life with all the velocity of a freakin' bullet.

20th November

I've read that email from Dylan a million times and I can't work out whether I should be hating his guts or still pining after him. I think the pining will win out in the end. I saw him the day after he sent it as I was standing outside the café waiting for Anna to open up.

He came out of Rhythm with a mug of coffee, which he handed to me.

'What's this for?' I asked him, but it wasn't in a bitchy way, I was just curious.

'It's too cold to wait outside,' he murmured, pulling his jumper closer around him. 'Thought you might need something to warm you up.' The annoying thing was he didn't even sound remotely leery.

'Thanks,' I said. I took a sip of coffee and tried not to pull a face. Dylan makes terrible coffee. He can never get the right ratio of Kenco, hot water and milk.

'Did you get my email?' he demanded after an awkward pause that seemed to last several millennia.

I nodded.

'So . . .' Dylan prompted.

I took another sip of coffee, mainly for something to do with my mouth that didn't involve speaking. 'It sort of knocked me for six,' I said eventually. 'I'm still deciding what I think about it.'

Dylan got quite agitated then. Started shuffling his feet and moving closer to me, like he was going to touch me. I stepped out of his reach. 'But did you . . . ?'

God! What was his problem? 'I'll get back to you, Dylan,' I snapped. Really snapped. Even *I'd* never heard that kind of edge to my voice before. 'Just leave it, will you?'

He turned and walked back into Rhythm without saying another word. And slammed the door just for good measure.

I got Poppy to return the empty mug.

7th December

I've been the busiest of little bees. I've volunteered to help out at the local hospital's children's ward Christmas Party thing. It wasn't even Mum's idea. And I'm not doing it because it will look good on my UCAS form. There was a notice up at college and Nat and I decided we should 'give something back'. And possibly meet some good-looking medical students. Which is just me being glib because actually hanging out with some ill kids who might not even make it through to Christmas puts everything in perspective. And keeps me occupied.

12th December

I've spent all day making Christmas decorations with the kids. It was actually very cool. They think I'm, like, a proper adult. One of them asked me if I was thirty. Note to self: Look into anti- ageing creams.

But it's also kind of depressing. One of the kids, Asha, is so poorly she just lies in bed and hardly moves. I went and sat with her and made her a little angel to put on her medical chart.

Nat and I are going to do a collection at college to

raise some money to buy them all a Christmas present. I think I'm finally getting a social conscience.

14th December

I bumped into Shona and Dylan in town. On a scale of one to ten of sheer awfulness, it was only about an eleven.

'Hello stranger,' was Shona's greeting when I collided with them as I was going into Paperchase and they were coming out.

'Oh, hi,' I muttered. 'Um, hey Dylan.'

'Edie,' he said, shoving his hands into the pocket of his coat. He had a really cool Big Black Records hat on and his face was pink with the cold.

'Where you been hiding?' Shona asked as we stepped to one side so we weren't getting in the way.

I started telling them about helping out at the hospital. God, I talked for England. Then when I got on to the subject of Asha, I began to cry. I just couldn't help it. 'Cause it's Christmas and she's just a little kid and she's got cancer which sucks beyond the telling of it.

'I'm sorry,' I spluttered. 'Just ignore me.'

'Do you want to get a coffee?' Shona squeezed my hand. 'We're just done, aren't we, Dylan?'

Dylan nodded. 'Don't cry, Edie,' he murmured, stroking my wet cheeks with the back of his hand, which just made me cry harder. 'Maybe you should give the hospital a miss today.'

They were both giving me concerned looks and

tilting their heads to the side. I dug in my coat pockets for a slightly grubby tissue and wiped my eyes. 'No, I have to go. I'm just, y'know, Christmas and PMS and sick children. Not a good combination.'

'Well, I don't . . .' Shona began to say but I gave her a quick hug and picked up the bags I'd put on the pavement.

'I need to get going,' I said quickly. 'I'll see you soon. OK?' And I dashed off as Dylan shouted something about a Christmas party at me.

17th December
Today I deleted the email from Dylan because I need to stop reading it every hour and theorising about what every word means. All that stuff he wrote about me being heartless and hard has really wounded me. I have too much heart, if anything. It gets me into trouble all the time.

18th December
It was the Christmas Party at the children's ward today. One of the doctors dressed up as Father Christmas and we sang carols and handed out presents.

Nat and I managed to raise just under thirty quid and my dad rounded it up to fifty. We bought all the kids a book and one of those stockings stuffed full of chocolate each. Aw! In return we got this home-made card that they'd all signed with a picture of me and

Nat on it (I had yellow hair, I was pleased to see) by a Christmas tree. I think it was a Christmas tree. Either that, or a really strange-looking reindeer.

I sat and held Asha's hand for a little bit and she tried to sit up. Her parents were there and they thanked me for making the angel and for spending time with her. Her mum seemed really reined in, like she was trying to hold herself together and when I went to say goodbye and gave Asha a kiss on the forehead, her mum hugged me so hard, I thought she was going to break one of my ribs.

19th December
Asha died last night.

20th December
Nat has gone down in history as the only boy who's ever going to be allowed to spend the night in my room. I phoned him in tears yesterday to tell him about Asha and he came over and we both cried a lot and ate too many mince pies.

And then I asked if he could stay over and Mum went and got a pair of Dad's pyjamas for him to sleep in and then I laughed so hard that I was one pelvic floor exercise away from completely wetting myself.

The only other person that I really wanted to call was . . . not on my speed dial any more.

23rd December

Nat and I spent the day delivering our Christmas cards. He's all about being busy to take our minds off being sad about Asha and depressed about toxic ex-boyfriends. The postman thing didn't take very long actually. But it did take an hour for him and Shona (who was the only other person on our delivery route) to persuade me to go round to Dylan's new flat.

'So we'll just pretend that we were passing,' Shona said.

'We've got to deliver some Christmas cards anyway,' Nat reckoned.

'But we *are* just passing. And we do have to deliver Christmas cards,' I pointed out as they dragged me up the garden path.

I had never been privileged enough to actually get an invitation to Dylan's home when we were, like, dating but there I was standing nervously on his doorstep with Nat and Shona each grabbing one of my arms so I couldn't make a run for it.

Paul answered the door and led us into the lounge. I thought I was going to throw up. There was Dylan with Veronique sitting on his lap. Do they have to be surgically attached to each other all the time? Then there was Simon, who I hadn't seen since I got drunk and ended up snogging him, and that lanky git Carter who looked up and said, 'Oh, it's Eddie, no longer an officially missing person.'

'Oh it's Cartman,' I hissed. 'The rudest boy in the world.'

'It's *Carter*, sweetheart,' he said.

'And it's *Edie*, dickweed,' I snarled while Shona shot me a warning look.

I had to sit there for a very painful hour while Veronique wittered on about her Performance Art piece. I don't know what Dylan sees in her. He kept sneaking looks at me like he couldn't believe that I was sitting there on his sofa after my disappearing act. I pretended everything was cool but seeing him with Veronique tore me apart. And what with Simon's smirking and Carter's sneering the whole thing was just horrible.

Dylan asked me how the children's party had gone when he finally came up for air and all I could do was shrug while Shona made 'shut your mouth right the hell now' motions at him.

He didn't get it. And finally Nat bellowed, 'It was fine, OK? Can we talk about something else now?'

I don't think we're going to be invited back there any time soon.

25th December

Christmas sucks. Fact. The grand'rents were doting on me and I even got a sweet silver pendant from Tiffany's as my big present, which was all kinds of good. Then I realised that Dylan had been dating Veronique for longer than he'd dated me. And all the Quality Street and mixed nuts in the world couldn't change that. I'd got a Christmas card from him the day before. Another charming message:

Dear Edie
Even you can't keep the silent treatment going all of next year too, can you? I'm not going to wait forever.
D x

Because 'Merry Christmas and a happy new year' would have just been too bloody simple.

1st January
The New Year started with a bang and an 'Oh dear' and very possibly a 'Bloody hell' too. Nat had promised that we'd stay in until he heard that Trent was in town and going to the lads' party. I absolutely refused to go but, after tears and tantrums and Nat threatening to tell everyone we knew that it actually said Edith on my birth certificate, there I was hiding behind Dylan's Crimbo tree/art installation/whatever in my new vintage cocktail dress and wishing I wasn't.

I was just helping myself to another glass of punch when Dylan came up behind me.

'Hey,' he muttered.

'Hey,' I said.

'The card . . .' he trailed off.

'Was another of your little mind games,' I finished for him.

'Look, Edie, I just want to be friends with you . . .' He said it so smooth as well, like he was the most reasonable boy on the planet.

Just to have him standing there in his stupid jeans and his stupid Trash T-shirt filled me with an indescribable fury. Which made me want to hurt him like he always managed to hurt me. I was fed up with being miserable and moping after him. And I was so, so, so sick of the way that he'd act like me being mad at him was silly. I'd made a rational and sanity-protecting decision to keep away from him and he should have respected that. Plus, the sight of him and her together always made me want to yak all over the floor.

'Why don't you get it, Dylan?' I asked and my voice was as cold as the ice cubes in my drink. 'I don't want to have a friend like you. Y'know, friends implies that you actually get on with someone and you want to spend time with them and they make you feel good about yourself. And, hey, when it comes to me and you – none of the above apply.'

Finally I'd said it and the fact that his face sort of crumpled at least meant that the message was beginning to sink in. Or so I thought until he said, 'You don't mean that.'

He tried to stroke my arm but I flinched away from him and then he attempted the whole staring into my eyes routine but I've grown a pair since last year. 'God, were you even listening to me?' I exclaimed angrily. 'Just leave me alone.'

Dylan was definitely pouting now and I was at a loss to fathom out why an Edieless existence was something that he had such trouble coming to terms with and that's when it hit me.

'You might be going out with *her*, you might be sleeping with her but I bet you can't get me out of your head,' I announced triumphantly. 'That's what this is all about. You still want me!'

My raised voice had cleared the kitchen and Dylan shifted uncomfortably.

'When you talk like that Edie,' he was saying, 'I'm so glad we're not going out any more.'

I felt like he'd punched me in the stomach.

'No you don't,' I insisted, forgetting the whole get out of my life and don't let the door hit you in the arse speech of five minutes ago. 'I know you still want me.'

'Yeah, like a freakin' hole in the head.'

Something had changed. Dylan was the hunted and I was like the hunter. I reached up and kissed him. He tried to hold back but for one delicious moment he gave in, really gave in and kissed me back so passionately that I knew that whatever he had with Veronique, didn't come close to what he had with me. Then he was pushing me away.

'I can't do this to her,' he mumbled and walked out.

There was the sound of a slow handclap from the doorway. I whirled round to see Carter standing there.

'What do you do for an encore?' he wanted to know.

'How long were you standing there?' I demanded.

'Long enough.' He slowly looked me up and down. 'I haven't known you for very long, but are you always such a bitch?'

'What's it to you?' It was like some evil demon had taken me over. I was drunk on my own Dylan-seducing power.

'Veronique's my sister,' Carter said very calmly. 'If you mess with her, you mess with me.'

I pushed past him. 'Ooooh! I'm really scared – not!' was my parting shot.

He caught up with me in the lounge as the count-down to midnight started. 'You really are a little cow,' he said tauntingly. 'What did Dylan ever see in you?'

I'm hazy about what happened next. I think I called him a stickboy loser and then we were kissing but it was total war. Eventually we came up for air. I scraped a hand across my tingling mouth and looked at him.

'Well, it's one way to shut you up,' Carter said a little unsteadily.

There was a collective gasp and I looked round to see everyone, including Dylan, looking at me and Carter in shocked silence.

4th January

Everything has changed! I'm so on to Dylan now. If I push him just far enough in the right direction, I can have him back. Then once I've got him, I can turn around and mess with his head, just like he's messed with mine.

But I'm not that kind of girl. I wish I was. I wish I could be all calculating and cruel and focussed on my plans for revenge but . . . but . . . I was doing so well at the getting over him. And I know that pursuing him and making him dump Veronique for me would only store up some really bad relationship karma for myself.

So, tempting as the idea is of totally playing him, I'm going to pass. And just carry on keeping him out of my life.

Oh who the hell am I kidding?

17th January

I am a bad, bad person. I'm, like, irredeemably bad. But I know, I just *know* that he still loves me and he still wants me and he still wants to be with me. I'm absolutely sure of it. Even though after the New Year argument and kissage, Dylan has tried to make it abundantly clear (by which I mean avoiding the café and *crossing to the other side of the road if he sees me coming!*) that he doesn't want me around. But I don't believe him, which is why I seem to get this sadistic kick out of cornering him so he can't escape, and then flirting shamelessly with him The weirdest thing is that this evil behaviour is not my style. And while I'm watching Dylan, Carter is watching me and trying to keep me away from his sister's boyfriend.

Tonight, I ended up wedged next to Dylan on Shona's sofa as we watched *The Virgin Suicides* for, like, the sixtieth time. Veronique was rehearsing one of her crappy Performance Art pieces someplace else and the lights were dim as I ran my finger lightly down Dylan's arm. It's not what I really wanted to do. The urge to wrap myself around him and feel his ribs against my side and his heart beating was so strong, it made my skin twitch. I know it's wrong to make passes at other girls' boyfriends, I do. But he was mine long before he was hers. And I could feel the way his arm itched to curl round me. I grabbed his hand and stroked his palm longingly.

'Cut that out,' Dylan hissed at me, pulling his hand away.

I shifted restlessly from my cramped position on the end of the settee.

'And stop wriggling like that!' Then he pushed me so I found myself sitting on the floor! I glared at him.

Dylan shrugged and looked utterly unrepentant. 'I'm trying to watch the film, Edie. And you keep fidgeting.'

I rested my head on my knees and wondered why in a room crammed with people, I could feel so alone. To make matters worse, I was sitting next to Carter who smiled nastily and muttered, 'Ha! Foiled again.'

I don't think I've ever hated anyone as much as I hate him.

20th January

Dylan never comes into the café on his own any more. But I caught him out today. I'd popped in on my way home to pick up my wages when I saw him sitting at the corner table. I walked over and kissed him on the cheek in a friendly fashion. He didn't look very pleased to see me.

'Oh, it's you,' he said.

'Can this be the same Dylan who wrote me a letter saying, what was it?, "I miss your kisses and how right it felt to hold you."' My voice went all trembly.

Dylan didn't look at me. 'New Year changed everything.'

'I know.' My hand hovered in the air because I wasn't allowed to touch him. 'I realised that you still love me and I still love you.'

He sighed then, like I'd said something hurtful. 'You have to move on, Edie.'

'What if I can't?'

As I stood there and watched him trace patterns in the sugar bowl with his finger; noted the way his hair flopped into his eyes; the rigid, set lines of his face, he seemed so distant. Like he'd never ever been close to me.

Dylan looked up and stared at me for a second without speaking. 'Don't make me end up hating you,' he said, but sadly, like he knew that even as he said it, he was lying and he did still love me.

I stumbled out of the door almost blinded by tears and bumped into Carter.

'Oh, well if it isn't the relationship wrecker,' he said cheerily.

It wasn't worthy of retaliation and, besides, I was way too close to completely losing it. I just pushed him out of the way – hard – and ran.

23rd January
So, like, there I was, minding my own business and trying to write a French essay on drug addiction, when I heard The Mothership calling me.

I stuck my head round the bedroom door to see Veronique coming up the stairs!

'What do *you* want?' I asked her in a horrified voice. Like, the enemy had invaded my territory.

'I wanted to talk to you,' she said in her stupid, girly voice. She always sounds like she's been sucking on helium.

I stood on the landing, barring the way to my bedroom, with my arms folded across my chest. 'About what?'

'About Dylan and about Jake,' she said hesitantly but I wasn't buying the little girl lost act for a second.

I frowned. 'Who's Jake?'

She rolled her eyes. 'Y'know, my brother.'

'Oh, Carter! Well what about him?' I asked her.

She gave me a slow once-over and I wished I wasn't wearing a ratty pair of pyjama bottoms and a vest that had gone grey in the wash. She was definitely winning in the style stakes especially as she was wearing the polka dot skirt that I'd nearly bought in H&M the other week. 'Look, it's bad enough that you keep flirting with Dylan but all Jake talks about is you. It's all, "I saw Edie yesterday," or "Edie likes the Beatles too."' Her voice rose perilously high at the end of the sentence.

'OK, I'll admit the stuff about Dylan,' I spluttered. 'I'm not going to apologise because you could never understand about me and Dylan. As for Carter, I hate him, he hates me. End of story. And I have a French essay to write so could you please leave?'

As I turned away, I heard her say: 'You know the really sad thing? You and I could have been such good friends but if this is the way you want it, so be it.'

'Is that meant to be a declaration of war or something?' I demanded, whirling round.

Veronique threw me a look of utter hatred. 'I guess so! And you are not going to know what's hit you.'

30th January

I thought I'd be dodging scud missiles and stuff

but Veronique's call to arms has obviously gone unnoticed. Well, 'cept Dylan has started getting his lunch from Pret A Manger.

And Shona never calls but we haven't really been close for a while, which is a pity because I miss her.

5th February

Veronique is such a bitch! It was Dylan's birthday yesterday (I sent him a card and a mix CD I'd made but he didn't text me back when I left a message asking if he'd got them) and she had a party for him and didn't even invite me. Which, yeah, fair enough. But she invited Nat, who's my friend. And she even invited Poppy from the café. Nat didn't go though he offered to poke his head in so he could bring me the gossip. Then he got an attack of conscience and came round and listened to me rant on and on for, like, hours. He told me I was becoming a 'scary obsesso girl'. Although Poppy went she was so useless at relaying the important details, like what Veronique was wearing and whether her and Dylan were all over each other.

'They were together but not together together, if you know what I mean,' was her very disappointing summing up of the evening. Then, when I scowled, she very sweetly and sarcastically told me that next time I should send her off with a questionnaire and she'd tick the boxes for me.

14th February

Three Valentine cards! That has to be a record. I know one's from Nat 'cause it has Hello Kitty on it. The other two cards are arty ones. I hope beyond hope that the one with a Georgia O'Keefe flower is from Dylan but it doesn't have any handwriting on, just a heart with my name in the middle in capitals.

The other one is very strange. It has a bleeding heart on the front and I don't recognise the writing at all. 'Even amid fierce flames, a golden lotus can be planted,' my mystery admirer had written.

I hate cryptic stuff. It makes my head hurt.

16th February

Shona rang! They're all going to Southport this weekend and she wanted to know if I was up for it.

I was really restrained. I didn't automatically ask if Dylan was going, even though I haven't seen him to speak to for a month and I have the worst withdrawal symptoms.

But God, I'll even go to Southport for the day on the remote chance that he might be going too.

And, for future reference, no, I don't really like this sad girl I've become.

21st February

I never got to Southport. Not after Veronique had arranged who was going in whose car, so there was no room for me. I felt about *this* big. Paul and Shona had already left and I had to stand and pretend that I hadn't wanted to go anyway.

'I can get three people in the back of . . .' Dylan trailed off and wouldn't look at me.

Veronique smirked. 'Sorry Edie, maybe next time,' she simpered, winking at the two sappy friends she was with.

I turned and walked away without a word. It wasn't fair, Veronique was winning. I was just contemplating throwing myself under the first bus that came along, when there was a tug on my sleeve. It was Carter. My joy was now complete.

'What do you want?' I gulped because I was trying so hard not to cry.

'It's OK, I haven't come to gloat,' he said with a strange little smile. 'Well, maybe just a little.'

I shot him a look and carried on walking. Carter fell into step beside me.

'Why aren't you on your way to Southport with your stupid sister?' I spat out after five minutes.

He ignored that comment. 'So where are you going?'

I shrugged. 'Going home. Placing an ad. Finding some new friends.'

'I'm your friend,' Carter said softly.

'Are you on crack? You and I are about as close to being friends as I am to . . . to . . .' But I couldn't think of any metaphor large enough to contain the notion that we were mates. I still wanted to cry so shutting up seemed like a really good idea. We got to my bus stop and I pretended to scrutinise the timetable like it was about to tell me the secrets of the universe. There was another tug on my sleeve and I couldn't help but glance at his face. Carter was twisting the signet ring he wears and eyeing me up. I mean, he was definitely eyeing me up. Looking at my lips and then his eyes moved downwards in the direction of my chest, though, quite frankly, there's nothing much to see there, even without a tightly buttoned-up jacket over it.

And the really annoying thing was that I started blushing. I just couldn't help it.

Y'know, he'd just checked me out. And he was still checking me out and I was still blushing and, we were, like, having a moment.

'So . . . d'you want to go to the cinema this evening?'

'Are you asking me out?' I spluttered.

He looked me dead in the eye. 'Yeah.'

What the hell?

21st February (later)

Tonight was very . . . I don't think there's a word in the dictionary that could even come close to describing it.

I've never met anyone like Carter before. It was weird because we did actually get on even though we

78

argued all the time. We argued about what film to go and see and who was going to pay for the tickets and where we were going to sit. It was a regular old bickerfest, but it was kinda enjoyable. Whatever . . .

And he's twenty-three (he's doing a postgraduate art thingy) and I'm not even eighteen yet. He wears sharp second-hand suits that always have splashes of paint on them. His hair is dark blond and quiffed and he looks like he's stepped out of an old black-and-white film. He's bony in this elegant way and it always seems as if he's either a) laughing at some private joke that no-one else gets or b) quietly seething. Halfway through the film, after our hands kept colliding in the popcorn bucket, Carter pulled me towards him and started to kiss me. Gentle kisses that made me want him to grab me and throw me down on the floor and do things to me that I could never, ever tell anyone about. And just when I thought he was going to, he stopped and settled back down to watch the film.

'You should pay attention,' he whispered in my ear. 'I'll be asking questions later.' Carter was not a relaxing person to be around.

Afterwards we went for a drink in the pub at the corner of his road.

'You're such a funny little thing,' he said, laughing as my awkward silence default setting kicked in. Just when I was finally starting to relax and wonder if he'd kiss me again, Dylan slid into the seat opposite!

'What are you doing here?' Carter and I both asked, though he sounded really pissed off whereas I couldn't keep the delight out of my voice. It was Dylan and me sharing the same breathing space.

Dylan pulled a face. 'Your sister decided to stay in Southport with the others but I've got to work tomorrow.' His eyes narrowed. 'Anyway what are you two up to?'

'Nothing,' I said too quickly while Carter murmured something about the cinema.

Dylan stood up. 'Whatever!' he said in a suspicious voice. 'I might as well walk you home.'

Carter raised an eyebrow. 'It's OK, Dylan, I'm already on it.'

'It's completely out of your way,' hissed Dylan, turning to me. 'C'mon, you're going home.'

I sat there watching them argue over chaperone duties until Dylan grabbed me and my coat and pulled me out of the door.

We walked most of the way in this tense silence. I was trying to process what had just happened but I was at a loss to come up with anything that made any sense.

'What was all that about?' I finally demanded.

Dylan gave me a furious look. 'You're so stupid Edie,' he bit out angrily. 'Carter doesn't fancy you, he just wants to keep you out of my way. Can't you tell when you're being used?'

I shook his hand off my arm. 'What's it to you? You don't care about me.'

'Yes I do,' insisted Dylan.

We were at my gate. 'You've got a funny way of showing it,' I said as I fumbled for my key. 'You make me feel like I'm completely worthless.'

Dylan and I locked eyes and then he held out his arms and I stumbled into his embrace. It had been so long that I'd almost forgotten how good it felt when he held me and how his kisses were another reason for living.

But all too quickly Dylan was backing away from me. He ran a finger down the side of my face. 'Keep away from Carter, Edie, he's bad news.' Then he turned and walked away.

If I think about this any more, my head might explode.

23rd February

Neither of them have called. Why am I even surprised?

28th February

Went to see a band with Poppy. We were talking about our chef, Italian Tony, and whether he was actually Italian or just had a speech impediment, when I looked up and saw Carter at the bar.

'Who's that?' asked Poppy.

I managed to tear my eyes away. 'Some boy who's been trying to mess with my head.'

Poppy rolled her eyes and gave me a nudge. 'Oh, Edie, you can be so melodramatic sometimes.'

I couldn't concentrate on the band or their foxy singer, it was as if Carter had a special Edie radar fitted.

I managed to shimmy subtly in his direction but he didn't say hello or acknowledge me in any way. I so don't need to start getting obsessed with another boy.

3rd March

Nat had big news when I met him for lunch today. Seems like Dylan and Veronique had a furious row on Saturday night about a backdrop he'd painted for one of her stupid Performance Art pieces and now they're not talking. Hah!

5th March

Dylan came into the café today and asked me what I was doing tonight! I was like, 'Oh so you've remembered that I exist then?' He gave me one of his looks and it had been so long since he'd arched an eyebrow in my direction and given me one of his slow-simmer smiles that I arranged to hang out with him tonight. That's how he phrased it; 'So do you wanna hang out after work?'

I'm so bloody happy that he's talking to me and he wants to spend time with me, that I'm not thinking rationally at all. 'Cause am I like just being really sad and taking after my glamorous Aunt Glo who reads books with titles like *Women Who Love Too Much*? Maybe I should be stronger and not so much of a pushover. Y'know, Dylan blows hot and cold and hurts me terribly on a weekly basis and then as soon as he crooks a finger, I come running.

Not only that, I have a sneaking suspicion I'm totally mixing my metaphors.

5th March (but later)

It was so near to being a proper date that I thought I might just as well call it one. I got home, had a thirty-second shower and threw every item of clothing I had onto the floor before settling for a vintage flowery dress, my motorcycle boots and a headscarf/pigtails combo. Well, it's a look.

And Dylan was wearing *his* motorcycle boots, jeans and one of his really dodgy second-hand shirts. This one was cream with little pink stripes running down it. God, I don't know where he finds them. I think all the little old ladies who work in the local charity shops must put them to one side for him. '*What a revolting garment, Gladys. That lanky boy with the scruffy hair is bound to buy it, why don't you mark it up to a fiver?*'

Dylan always sees right inside me, no matter how

much bullshit I come up with. I ended up confessing how sad I was that me and Shona had drifted apart and how I felt like, apart from Nat and maybe Poppy, I didn't have any real friends any more.

We tried really hard not to talk about Veronique but Dylan made this snarky remark about how nice it was to go out with a girl who didn't expect him to pay for every round. I shouldn't have felt ridiculously pleased, but I did.

We had a few drinks in the pub and Dylan wanted to go to this new Sixties garage night at a club in town. It was, like, we couldn't say what we really wanted to say, which was that neither of us wanted to go home just yet. So we skirted round it with this whole, 'You could come along, if you want', 'If you're sure you don't mind' crap.

When we got to the club I forced Dylan to dance even though he protested and eventually he disappeared to get some drinks. Watching him walk back across the dancefloor, his gaze so intently on me, made my heart ache.

'Being with you makes me want to cry,' I said as he sat down next to me.

He put an arm round me and I nuzzled my face against the cosy spot where his neck and shoulder met. 'I've missed your Edieisms,' he muttered. 'And I've missed you. There's been so many times when I wanted to ring you but you were out of bounds.'

'You could have called me,' I cried. 'Nothing's changed.'

Dylan squeezed my hand. 'Everything's changed.'

'Oh, please kiss me,' I begged because I knew that it would make everything all right.

I ended up sitting on Dylan's lap with my hands in his hair and his lips on mine. It would've been perfect if someone hadn't decided to chuck beer all over me. I looked up to see Veronique with an empty pint glass in her hand.

'How could you?' she screamed at Dylan. 'With that creature!'

I didn't stick around. I scrambled off Dylan and nearly knocked her over in my haste to get away.

So there I was walking the streets of Manchester, cold, wet, stinking of beer and unable to find an empty cab. Getting abducted would just about finish off a perfect evening I thought as a car drew up alongside me. It was Carter.

'Get in,' he bit out.

'I'm all right,' I mumbled.

'Don't make me get out and put you in the car, Edie.'

I got in.

We didn't talk for a while. Carter was handling his gear lever very aggressively, like he wished it were my neck.

'You're unbelievable!' he suddenly shouted. 'What

is your problem?' I realised he must have been in the club with Veronique.

'Will you stop shouting at me,' I whispered.

'You couldn't leave him alone, could you?' he hissed, pulling over and switching off the engine.

'So? Why do you have to get involved in Veronique's love-life?' I said nastily. 'I guess it's more interesting than your own.'

'What would you know about it?'

'I know that you took me out and then ignored me,' I spat at him.

He grabbed my shoulders. 'I took you out,' he said slowly. 'Then watched you leave with *him.*'

Less than half an hour ago I'd been all over Dylan but suddenly I wanted Carter to kiss me. Desperately, I closed the gap between us and pressed my lips against his. Carter tried to pull away but I wound my arms round him and he kissed me back. It was different to kissing Dylan. Carter tasted different, he held me tight like he was frightened that I'd bolt and he was the one who pulled away first. I tried to kiss him again but he held me off.

'You should have a government health warning stamped on your head,' he told me before starting the car.

9th March
I must have texted Dylan like fifty times in the last

three days and he hasn't replied to any of them. Which, I guess, is his little way of telling me that he got back together with Veronique.

I might've phoned Carter if I'd had his number. Or maybe I wouldn't. I'm not quite sure what's going on there. I mean, if the Dylan thing was never, ever going to happen, then I'd probably be in the market for a new boyfriend but I'm not really sure if Carter would be my first choice. Or my second. Or even my third. But the Dylan thing was kind of happening again. And I'm not even sure that I *like* Carter or that he likes me. All I am sure of is that he's a really good kisser.

15th March

So, last night I was sure I heard a phone ringing but I thought it was part of my dream where I was helping my dad save the world from a terrorist threat. But when I woke up this morning, there was this long, rambly and, quite frankly, deeply disturbing message from Dylan on my voicemail. Time of call: 3.57 in the morning: 'Edie? God, I shouldn't be calling you . . . it's late . . . I'm drunk. I just . . . you know . . . I'm not a bad person but I'm treating you like shit and I just want you to know if I could get out of this thing with Veronique I would. It's complicated. Well, she's complicated. Just wanna be with you, kiss you, get naked with you . . . God, I'm so drunk. So sorry to be such a bastard to you, you don't deserve it and I'm terrified that you're going to get so pissed off with me that you just give up and start seeing someone else. But not Carter 'cause he's a piece of work, he's a wanker, he is. Him and Veronique, both of them, Jesus, you wouldn't believe the half of it. I shouldn't . . . I miss you so much . . . wish you were here right now . . . Oh, hell . . . why am I doing this? . . .'

I don't know what it means, apart from giving me a certain validation that all my bad Dylan decisions were made with the belief that he did still want me. Which turns out to be true. Er, yay? And I don't understand the Veronique/Carter thing. The best I can come up with is that they're having some sort of incestuous affair, which ewwwww!

15th March (later)

I just got this text from Dylan: 'V drunk lst nite. Ignore ne clls frm me.'

You know, if he keeps yanking me back and forth like a freakin' yoyo, eventually my string is just going to snap.

21st March

Nat's got a date. And I'm pleased for him, really I am. Especially as the date is this cute boy he's been lusting over for weeks. But it's late Saturday afternoon and I should be getting ready to go out and have fun and instead I'm preparing to go to

Blockbuster to pick up some chick flicks for me and Mum to watch. And you know what else? It's my birthday today. I'm eighteen; it's meant to be a big bloody deal and Nat was going to cancel his date so we could go out to dinner but all he's talked about for the last two months is how dreamy Joe is, so I was really mature about it. Shona called me this morning but she's going to a rave in Blackpool tonight with 'the others' and there was no invitation forthcoming. And it's not like we're good friends any more so why should she be obliged to spend my birthday with me? But the thing that really hurts (we're talking about the same level of pain that you might get from having a limb amputated) is that Dylan hasn't sent me a card or phoned me or even texted me. I'm eighteen and I've got no-one to do anything with on my birthday. Am I such an awful person?

21st March (later)

Oh God! I bumped into Carter in the DVD rental shop. Luckily, I'd picked up *Amelie* and not something really girly and tragic, though I'd just been about to snatch up the last copy of *He's Just Not That Into You*, when I heard a cough behind me. 'So this is what you get up to on a Saturday night?' It was Carter.

Of course, he was returning some arty foreign film on his way out to do something incredibly exciting with all his incredibly exciting friends.

'Oh, it's you,' I brushed past him so I could get some ice cream.

'So, I hear you've been managing to stay away from Dylan,' Carter continued, following me. 'Or vice versa.'

'Go away,' I said between gritted teeth.

He leant against the freezer door, even though most boys know that you should never come between a girl and her Rocky Road. 'You were a bit more talkative last time I saw you,' he continued. 'When you weren't trying to shove your tongue down my throat.'

'Look, about that . . . I was upset, I didn't know what I was doing,' I mumbled.

'Whatever.'

That was it, time to go!

Carter trailed me to the back of the queue, while I stared ahead and willed everyone in front of me to hurry up.

'You always disappear when things get interesting,' he smirked.

'Or when you insult me,' I pointed out.

'Look I'll see you around, sweetheart,' Carter said, bending down to give me a kiss on the cheek before he sauntered off.

How could I have thought that there was even the remotest chance that we might get together when he's so utterly obnoxious?

But never mind him for the moment. When I got

home, there was a huge bunch of flowers on the doorstep. No joke, there were about a hundred white freesias wrapped up in pink paper with a ribbon and even before I opened the card I knew they were from Dylan. I'd once told him how they were my favourite flowers because they smelt so lovely but you never get that many for your money. They must have cost him a fortune.

It was another home-made card. A collage this time with French words and Sixties girls stuck all over it. 'I remember exactly what I was doing this time last year,' he'd written. 'I can't turn back the clock but I can wish you Happy Birthday. Love you, D xxx'

I was definitely sniffing when I opened the front door and Mum said Poppy had just called (I'd left my moby at home) and she was waiting in the Dry Bar for me with Atsuko and Darby, a couple of girls from college.

Mum was really cool about me bailing on our chick flick night. She sat on the edge of my bed as I was pulling on my going out jeans and crying at the same time.

'I wish you'd tell me what's wrong, sweetheart,' she said. 'Is it about the flowers?'

'It's boy stuff,' I choked out. 'Big, hairy boy stuff.'

And then I burst into tears even though if you cry on your birthday you're meant to have bad luck for the rest of the year and also, I'm meant to be an adult now. But Mum just patted the spot next to her and gave me this amazing cuddle and didn't bug me for further details. Plus, she let me borrow her art deco earrings.

I had a good time. I drank too much, got seriously chatted up by this guy who's in the Manchester City reserve team, and for a brief moment I thought it would be very funny to date a footballer and change my name to Chardonnay. Instead I ended up with a bag of chips and Poppy crashing at my house.

It was a pretty good way to end my birthday actually.

26th March

I went out with Dylan last night. Because I am the most stupid girl in the world. I'm like Dylan's personal, Edie-shaped doormat. He just phoned up and asked me out as if we'd never split up and Veronique didn't exist and I said yes.

He picked me up in his car and as soon as I got in, he grabbed me and kissed the hell out of me before driving to an old man's pub on the edge of Withington.

'So I guess you're still seeing Veronique then?' I asked in the middle of some really intense hand-holding. It involved lots of squeezing and stroking and even a bit of nibbling.

Dylan pulled a face. 'Why have I taken you so far out of town, you mean?'

'Have you even *thought* about chucking her?' I asked, my voice going all wobbly.

'It's complicated. She gets hysterical and Carter . . .'

'What about Carter?'

'Do you really like him?' Dylan demanded. ''Cause he just sees you as a challenge, that's all.'

'Don't, Dylan,' I said. 'You know I wouldn't be here with you if I was interested in him.'

Dylan opened his mouth like he was about to disagree with me but I pulled his arms around me and made him kiss me until neither of us could think straight.

1st April

I think April Fools' Day should be re-branded as National Edie Day. I ended up getting off with Dylan last night *in his car* in a dark corner of Morrisons car park. I'm like the Queen of Skanktown, population: 1.

5th April

I've decided that I miss being, well, girly. I never get to share my nail varnish and ogle slinky actor boys and do girl stuff any more.

So I've decided to have a sleepover. Even though I'm eighteen and should be beyond all that.

11th April

My sleepover was very odd. Shona obviously wanted to

be somewhere else and after making a few pointed remarks about love triangles, she disappeared. Atsuko, Poppy and Darby lounged on my bed and watched *Breakfast at Tiffany's* while Poppy's little sister Grace didn't say anything to anyone but tried on, like, all my clothes. Gossiping about boys was hard, too. 'I'm sneaking around with my ex-boyfriend but sometimes think I have an inexplicable crush on his girlfriend's brother,' wouldn't have gone down too well.

The doorbell rang. 'Maybe Shona's come back,' I said, ignoring Poppy's sarcastic, 'Oh goody.' As I started down the stairs. I could hear Carter asking The Mothership if I was in. I raced to the door.

'It's OK, I'm here,' I squealed.

'Edith! I thought it was girls only . . .'

I glared at her. 'Just go away!' I carried on glaring till she took the hint.

Carter was leaning against the porch door, smirking. 'Edith?' he enquired silkily. 'Sorry to interrupt your little tea party.'

I was horribly aware of my tartan pyjama bottoms and Miffy T-shirt.

'What do you want?' I asked sulkily.

'I heard on the vine that you were seeing Dylan again—'

'No I'm not,' I interrupted angrily. 'Who told you that? That's rubbish.'

Carter straightened up from his slouching position. 'Good. 'Cause I thought we should have another stab at it. Y'know go out somewhere, if you want to.'

I looked at him. He gave me a wicked grin that transformed his normally sulky face into something quite alluring and I could feel my heart start to pound. What was wrong with me?

''Kay.' I shrugged, as though I didn't really care.

Carter moved with devastating speed to press me up against the wall, cup my face in his hands and kiss the stuffing right out of me. There was definite tongue action, which was new territory for us.

'That should keep you going till next time,' he told me when we finally came up for air. He opened the door. 'Oh yeah and Edie, you don't need to lie to me, you just need to stop seeing Dylan. I'll be in touch about that date.'

'But I haven't . . .' I started but Carter had already left.

15th April

I've decided to stop all the boy angst. Instead I'm going to concentrate on A-level angst. Serious A-level angst. They're, like, *weeks* away. And I've been so busy sneaking around with Dylan and having bad, wrong thoughts about Carter, that I've done no revision.

I texted them both. In fact, I sent them the same message because occasionally I can be quite evil, when there's no-one around to realise. 'I'm going into hiber-nation to do A-level cramming until June 11. Don't even think about contacting me until then. Love Edie xxx' I don't believe in text speak – I think it's lazy and anyway I've been trying to study the finer points of English grammar all morning and I think it's starting to stick.

29th April

I'm trying hard to do some serious studying. It should be easy. I'm meant to be thinking about Shakespeare and memorising Psychology but all I can do is think about kissing Carter and kissing Dylan and worry that I'm turning into some boy-crazed harpy.

23rd May

Am in exam hell. Fact. Way too hideous to go into here but I did get one of Dylan's home-made cards today with a picture of the top of my head poking over a mound of books and papers. He wished me luck and although he didn't mention the other 'L' word anywhere he put kisses after his name. That has to mean something.

27th May

Was actually pleased to go into work today. It's the only social life I have at the moment. Poppy reckons that we should start a band after my exams are over. Ever since she found my old acoustic guitar under my bed at the sleepover she's been banging on about it. Even when I told her that I only managed, like, five lessons and then gave up, it didn't stop her from rehearsing her acceptance speech for when we win our first Brit award.

And did I mention that I think her psycho little sister Grace is stalking me? Every time I turn my head she seems to be there. Maybe she's working up to actually saying hello.

11th June

Had my last exam this morning. It was History and I think I did OK. Thank the Lord that my reckless decision to concentrate most of my revision energy on the Russian Revolution paid off. But as I was coming out of college who should be waiting for me but Carter, propped against the bonnet of his car, sunglasses on, smirk firmly attached to his face as I goggled at him. I was glad that I'd tried to make an effort for my last exam and was wearing my daisy-sprigged vintage dress.

Carter took my bag from me and slung it on the back seat and told me to get in.

We didn't speak until I realised that he wasn't taking me home.

'Where are we going?' I demanded.

He gave me an amused look. 'On that date. I've

been very patient waiting for you to finish your further education.'

'Well you could have called,' I muttered. 'Though I probably wouldn't have answered the phone.'

'Yeah, I could have . . .' he agreed and then he asked me how the exams had gone. We drove out to the countryside with sheeps and cows and stuff. Although he was being very obnoxious (even for him and that was saying something), Carter had got it together to make a picnic or, to be more exact, bought some crisps and biscuits and a bottle of wine. We sprawled out next to a stream and after I'd drunk some of the wine it seemed natural to curl up in his arms and doze off. I woke up when he started to kiss me. They were soft, languid kisses and although I could tell that he wanted more he didn't protest when I sat up and began to re-button my cardie.

He lay stretched out on the grass, the sun glinting on his blond hair, and I had to ruin everything by saying, 'So are we going out with each other?'

Carter casually waved one of his hands in the air. 'Let's keep it loose, honey,' he drawled. 'It ruins things when you have to put a name on them. Now come back here and give me a kiss.'

And when I wouldn't he said in a cold voice, 'It's not like you have Dylan any more. He's back with my sister but you'll find out about that.'

Then I got in a huff and made him get up and drive me home and I refused to speak to him. Sometimes I hate him so much. He can make everything go dark in, like, an instant.

13th June

Today was freaky with added bits of freakiness. Dylan and Veronique came round to see me at work and I had to stand outside on the street and have this, well, 'conversation' with them. Though I'm *so* using sarcastic quote marks.

I didn't even realise she was there. I looked up from the coffee machine to see Dylan walking towards me and giving me what I thought was a fiercely possessive look and my insides melted. Carter had just been bullshitting me and it was going to be all right because Dylan still fancied me. So, I hadn't seen him for two months? So what? Nothing had changed. Then I realised that Veronique was right behind him. And my insides stopped melting and hardened into this big, heavy ball that bounced around inside of me until I thought I was going to throw up.

Veronique did all the talking. Seems like Carter was right, they are back with a bang.

'And you thought I'd want to know because . . . ?' I asked her.

'Because you were the reason we almost split up in

the first place,' she replied sweetly. 'I know how you came onto him a few weeks ago. I know all about it, we don't have any secrets, do we Dylan?'

I waited for Dylan to tell her that *he'd* had something to do with that but he just raised his eyebrows and shrugged his shoulders like he didn't want to get involved.

'I'm not going to buy any of this crap about you and Dylan being friends. It's simple – if you try and break us up again, you're gonna have a really difficult summer,' Veronique continued. 'No Shona, no Paul, no Carter.'

I felt icy fingers clutch round my heart. 'You going to run me out of town, are you?' I managed to spit out.

Veronique's eyes flashed at me. 'I'm not messing Edie. I'm deadly serious.'

I looked to Dylan for support. 'There was never really anything between us,' he said quietly as if he was trying to believe it himself.

I tried to say something with my eyes. To convince him to tell her that they were over. To admit that he loved me, but he just wasn't tuning into my brainwaves.

'Do we have a deal?' Veronique asked.

I had nowhere left to run. I nodded my agreement.

16th June

Got this email from Dylan late last night:

To: cutiesnowgirl@hotmail.com
From: artboy@hotmail.com

I'm sorry.

D.

Well, I guess that's that then. I think he just broke the string on that yoyo of mine.

17th June

I'm going to work full-time at the café over the summer while I try to figure out what I'm doing with my life and wait for the no doubt disastrous A-level results to come out. I deferred entry on my UCAS form but I need a ridiculous number of points to get onto the course I want to do (French and Art History at University College London). So after summer's over, I'll probably have to do re-takes and then I can spend the rest of the year . . . I don't know, doing some crappy McJob and maybe saving up enough to go travelling. Nat muttered something about us going to South America for a few months but we're both a pair of princesses who could never stay in anything below a three-star hotel, so we'd probably have to save up a ton of cash.

I think it would be a good idea to try and heal my broken heart before September. I've tried to be good and restrained and not just blah blah blah on about

Dylan here but all I can do is go over stuff in my head when I should be sleeping. He's an emotional cripple. That's what glamorous Auntie Gloria would call him anyway.

21st June

I started full-time at the café yesterday so I get to muck around all afternoon with Poppy when she comes in to cover the lunchtime shift. I think she might be my new best friend. She's wicked cool and funny but there's something a little . . . detached about her. She always holds a little bit of herself back, which actually isn't a bad idea. And she's become obsessed with the idea of us starting a band.

She's been playing with boys (you know what I mean!) but she reckons they're all 'Sexist, talentless dweebs who think a girl's breasts get in the way of playing a guitar'. Maybe I can spend my gap year training to be a rock star? Or maybe not. Wouldn't go down well with the parents.

I suppose the really big news is that they're vacating the premises for two months. Dad's taking a sabbatical, though I call it being lazy, and they're going on a second honeymoon to Florida and taking a cruise. The weird thing is that they're quite happy to bugger off and leave me without a responsible adult around.

'*You're* meant to be a responsible adult,' Dad said drily when I pointed that out but Mum's already bought eight weeks' worth of ready-meals from Marks & Spencer's so she can be sure I won't live on fish fingers until they come back. The fact that making everything from all day breakfasts to oatmeal muffins is actually in my job description at the café has completely passed her by.

25th June

I got home after spending the day cleaning the café's hot plate to find Carter, the amazing vanishing boy, knee-to-knee with The Mothership over tea and scones.

When two different parts of your life collide and they're both giving you disapproving looks 'cause you're covered in griddle grease you find yourself wishing you had an elsewhere to be.

'Hard day at the office?' Carter grinned while my mum acted as if she was about to make me strip off there and then, like I was a messy toddler. I wouldn't put anything past her.

When I reappeared after scrubbing and changing, Carter jumped to his feet, he'd obviously reached Mother overload.

'Jake's going to take you to the cinema, isn't that nice?' she beamed at me.

I raised my eyebrows at Carter who threw me a challenging look. 'Well, it would have been nice if *Jake* had bothered to phone first,' I muttered.

'I thought we'd go and see a screening of *Lost In Translation* at the rep,' Carter said to me as he opened the car door for me. 'It seemed appropriate somehow.'

Of course, before the trailers even started Carter had his mouth locked onto mine and there it stayed for the next two hours. Then when we got outside he told me Veronique had invited us to dinner next Saturday before putting me in a taxi. Which is so many different levels of wrong that I can't even begin to go there.

30th June

I'm now lead guitarist of Poppy's all-girl band, Mellowstar while Atsuko and Darby from college are on drums and bass. They can't actually play but Poppy (who scares me with her ability to tune out anyone or anything that doesn't fit in with her musical master-plan) reckons that's a good thing as they haven't had time to develop any bad habits. And she thinks I'm a natural 'cause I can play the beginning of 'Super Bass' on my guitar. I'm *so* not.

1st July

Carter's just been on the phone to sort out our dinner date for tomorrow. I'd thought that the whole 'Veronique wants us to come for dinner' was one of his sick little jokes and I hadn't given it a moment's thought. Turns out it *was* Veronique's sick little joke and he was really insistent that I come. Like, we were dating or something and I was being a bitch because I didn't want to go round to his sister's. I wouldn't put it past her to lace my pasta with rat poison.

So I'm going. And it's not because Dylan will be there. I haven't written about him for twelve days, which only proves that my string is still well and truly snapped.

2nd July

Veronique's just had me for dinner, literally. When me and Carter got to her flat, Dylan nodded briefly in my direction once and then promptly ignored me. I ignored him back. With knobs on.

I gave Veronique the bottle of white wine I'd brought. 'I only drink red wine,' she said sweetly. 'But I guess I could use this for cooking.'

And although I'd phoned Carter to make sure she knew I didn't do green stuff, she'd made this hideous mung bean bake with salad. I tried to force it down by swallowing each mouthful with lots of water and a bit of dry heaving.

Then Carter and Dylan started arguing about British Art and Veronique kept saying stuff like, 'But I think that Tracey Emin provides a very powerful female presence.' The three of them acted like I wasn't there. They were being so pretentious and up themselves that I drifted off until I realised they were all staring at me.

'What?' I asked defensively.

'We were just wondering what you thought about the validity of Damien Hirst's latest work,' Veronique said. 'I can't wait to hear your views.'

He was the guy who pickled dead sheep, right?

'Um, he's quite cutting-edge, I s'pose,' I mumbled.

Carter gave me an encouraging smile. 'Go on . . .'

Veronique put a comforting hand on my arms, so comforting that I could feel her nails digging into me. 'I'm sorry Edie. I guess you're a little out of your depth. Why don't we talk about something you're into? Oh dear, I don't think I've ever watched *Hollyoaks*.'

'God, you sound just like my mum, Veronique,' I exclaimed innocently, earning myself a killer glare.

As I glanced up I almost drowned in Dylan's dark green eyes that were equal parts despair and longing as he pinned me to the chair with his gaze. I stared back, unable to stop myself, until Carter nudged me.

'Let's clear the table, shall we?' he said with an edge to his voice.

I grabbed some plates and hurried into the kitchen, followed by Carter who kicked the door shut.

'You're with *me*,' he hissed, pressing me up against the fridge. 'And don't forget it.'

And when Dylan came in five minutes later to get the dessert, I was wrapped round Carter like a clinging vine. There was only one way to get through the rest of the evening and it wasn't sober.

Carter had to stop the car on the way home so I could throw up. Didn't even hold my hair back for me either.

'I should have known you were too young to hold your drink,' he said nastily as he put me back in the car. Then he made me stick my head out of the window for the rest of the journey.

Somehow I think Carter's and my *thing* is drawing to a close.

7th July

Or not. I've seen Carter, like, every night this week. He refuses to call it a relationship. I think he just wants to get into my pants, quite frankly. And he's taken me to every art gallery in the 0161 area code. Quelle boring.

Just once, I'd like to find a boy I like and he likes me. We have a laugh and the kissing's really good and there's no-one getting in the way of the laughing and the kissing. Is that too much to ask for? Other people seem to manage it OK, so why can't I? I'm starting to think that I have an invisible radar on the top of my head that only art boys with severe emotional problems can pick up.

15th July

Waved the 'rents off really early. Crack of dawn kind of early. This second honeymoon thang is actually rather sweet, though it makes me slightly mopey 'cause at the rate I'm going I won't even be able to manage a first honeymoon. Even sweeter is the fact that they've left me unsupervised because they know I'm way too scaredy to even think about having a wild party. I'm slightly squicked out though at the thought of not having a designated adult on the premises especially when the house starts making those creepy intruder-on-the-stairs sound effects.

15th July (but later)
I can't believe what happened at work today! Anna suddenly announced that we're getting a new short-order cook in for the summer rush. Me and Poppy were getting really excited about the thought of working with some foxy super chef when Anna said, 'Oh, I think you know him, Edie. It's Dylan who works next door in Rhythm Records.'

I managed to get a grip on myself and muttered, 'Oh yeah, Dylan, that'll be nice.' But Poppy said afterwards that I'd rolled my eyes so strenuously she thought that my eyeballs had done a complete 360 degrees.

15th July (even later)
I don't know how I find time to even pee at the moment. After leaving work at five I managed to fit in

a quick band rehearsal with Poppy, Atsuko and Darby before rushing home to massage the cramp in my strumming hand and get ready to go out with Carter who took me to a gallery opening. It was very sophisticated (translation: pretentious). I stood there clutching a glass of white wine listening to loads of Carter's art boy mates waffling on about the artist's 'intense use of colour' when out of the corner of my eye I saw Dylan and Veronique snogging behind a post-modernist sculpture and I experienced my own intense use of colour. I saw red.

'What are you scowling about?' Carter enquired as he suddenly appeared at my side.

'All these people are so, so . . . so up themselves,' I spluttered 'cause I couldn't tell him the real reason why I was looking like I wanted to commit a double homicide. 'Whenever we go out you always take me to places stuffed full of really bad art installations.'

Carter closed his eyes very slowly and then opened them again. He does that a lot.

'So why don't you pick what we do next time?'

I gave him a slightly incredulous look. 'Oh, is there going to be a next time 'cause planning ahead would actually imply that we're in a relationship.'

'I think you actually have to be sleeping with someone for it to qualify as a relationship,' Carter murmured silkily into my ear and I could feel myself blushing.

Carter might not want to be my official boyfriend but he'd made it perfectly clear that he wouldn't be against getting pelvic with me.

'I want you to come to the college graduation party with me,' I said hastily, changing the subject.

'Oh no,' he groaned. 'I bet it will be full of sad girls training to be secretaries and boys doing electrical engineering.' He shuddered.

'I take it that's a no then?'

Carter just smiled and looped his arm round my shoulder before nudging me in the direction of Veronique and Dylan who'd finally come up for air. I so wished they hadn't because Dylan just stood there like one o'clock half struck and she managed to get, like, ten digs in in the course of a five minute conversation. They deserve each other.

15th July (much, much later)

I've just indulged in the sappiest behaviour ever known to girlkind. But when it's two in the morning and the hot water pipes sound *exactly* like a crazed nutter trapped in the wardrobe, you get so scared that you do stupid things like phoning your sort-of boyfriend and begging him to come over so he can look in previously mentioned wardrobe.

Carter took it well though he had a slight edge to his voice when he discovered the crazed nutter was actually a gurgling pipe.

'You sure it wasn't just an excuse?' Carter asked, after putting down the golf club I'd given him to use as a weapon.

'What?'

'You get me here and then have your wicked way with me,' Carter said hopefully.

I shuffled uncomfortably, suddenly aware of my pyjamas. I was naked under them! 'Yeah, in your dreams!'

'I could stay here while your parents are away, you know. See off any intruders, make sure their daughter's protected.'

I shook my head and grinned. 'Hmm and who's going to protect me from you?' I demanded as we walked down the stairs.

As I was opening the front door, Carter suddenly grabbed me and kissed me in a way that made my toes curl and my hands clutch at his shoulders to stop myself from falling over.

'Thought you might want to know what you were missing,' he chuckled as I pushed him through the door.

'Go!' I said firmly.

'I'll see you Monday night then,' Carter promised.

I frowned. 'Monday night?'

'The college graduation party,' he reminded me.

Sometimes I don't know whether to kiss him or kill him.

20th July

I always have a better time getting ready for a party than I do once I'm actually at the party and trying to be all party-like. Although it's just a college graduation bash and Carter's only coming with me 'cause I wore him down through the medium of nagging, I'm still really excited. So excited that I've spent most of the day in the hairdresser's blowing the emergency money Mum left me on some white blonde slices and a manicure. I don't know what I'm going to do if the hot water tank suddenly explodes but at least my hair looks all kinds of wonderful.

The reckless hair dye decision kind of inspired me and, as I stroked pink glittery varnish onto my toenails and wondered whether my matching hairslides and my pale pink Sixties shift dress were just a little *too* pink, I decided that tonight I was going to find my inner child and run with her. Forget being responsible and mature, tonight I was going to be irresponsible and *im*mature. I've spent far too much time recently being the queen of angst.

21st July

Carter turned up on time last night. Bang on time, which I don't think has ever happened before.

The doorbell rang as I was sliding on my cork wedges. I concentrated on walking sedately down the stairs and not breaking my neck even though the thought of getting to spend four hours with Carter was doing weird things to my stomach.

He had his hand raised to have another go on the doorbell when I finally managed to let him in. He was wearing narrow-legged trousers from one of his second-hand 1940s spiv suits and a short-sleeved shirt with little geometric patterns on it. Carter always looks like he'd been born sixty years too late. But in a good way.

'You took your time,' he complained, running a hand through his dark blond quiff.

'I was having trouble negotiating the stairs,' I muttered. 'I couldn't decide whether to go for functionality or fashion forwardness in my footwear.' Carter can still make me really nervous, even after all this time. Being nervous makes me talk a lot.

He looked me up and down. Slowly, I could feel a blush starting at my hairline and travelling all the way down to my newly varnished toes.

'I see fashion forwardness won in the end,' he commented archly. 'Can you walk in those?'

'Pretty much.'

'So am I coming in or are you actually ready, for the first time in our short but eventful relationship?' he asked. 'You look nice, by the way. Like a strawberry milkshake.'

'Oh thanks, Carter,' I said sullenly.

'I love strawberry milkshake!' he protested with a

smirk. 'Stop being so touchy. Now have you got everything: keys, purse, lip-gloss, phone . . . ?'

'I'm good to go,' I said decisively. 'Are you driving?'

'I thought we'd walk into town. I guess I should have checked the footwear situation with you first,' he smiled. 'We'll flag down a taxi once we get onto the main road.'

As I wobbled down the street in my wedge heels, Carter took my elbow. He doesn't do holding hands. In fact, he scorns all public displays of affection, unlike Dylan who'd been happy to snog me at bus stops and in shop doorways. But Dylan was the past and Carter was right now and I didn't even want to think about any possible boy-shapes that might be lurking in the future.

The party was being held at Kudos, this horrible, tacky nightclub in the centre of town.

As Carter caught sight of the two bouncers on the door and the gang of lads in pastel shirts, who were queuing to get in and stinking of cheap aftershave, he winced.

'I can't believe I let you talk me into this,' he said.

'Wait till you get inside then,' I teased. 'They have plastic palm trees and a dancefloor that lights up.'

'One of your regular haunts is it?'

'One of the chefs at work had his birthday party here,' I explained. 'There was a massive fight and I saw this guy get glassed. It was horrible and his girlfriend was crying because there was blood on her dress and . . .'

'Edie,' said Carter warningly. 'I'll give it an hour and if it sucks we're going.'

'Look, this is the end of two years of my life,' I told him as the bouncers unclipped the velvet rope and let us through. 'You could at least pretend that you want to be here. Not everyone can be as cool as you are.'

'That's for sure,' he remarked. 'What do you want to drink? One of those disgusting alcopops that you seem to love so much?'

I nodded and he disappeared in the direction of the bar.

Standing on my own in a nightclub is not one of my favourite occupations. I tried to assume a nonchalant I'm-just-waiting-for-all-of-my-best-friends-to-come-back-from-the-loo pose but I was sure everybody was staring at me and thinking that I was a complete loser who had no mates.

Suddenly I felt two hands squeeze my waist and I started in surprise.

'All right, Ediekins?' Nat said, by way of a greeting. 'You look delicious. Like a strawberry milkshake. I want to drink you all up.'

I turned round and nestled against him. 'I'm so glad you're here. I feel all out of sorts,' I said.

I love cuddling Nat. Not only does he always smell

really nice but I never have to worry that he'll get the wrong idea about me or that bits of him might start digging into me. Because ewwwww!

'You can pretend to be with me if you like but if I pull you're on your own,' Nat offered because he's all heart.

'I'm here with Carter,' I said darkly. 'But I'm not sure it was a good idea. I don't think he's in a party mood and he wants to go in, like, an hour.'

'Oh, your older man,' said Nat snidely, rolling his eyes.

'He's only twenty-three,' I snapped defensively. 'Five years is so not an age gap.'

'It is when he spends half the time acting like your dad. There's something creepy about him.'

'He's all right when you get to know him,' I insisted. 'He's really funny.'

'Funny peculiar,' said Nat, determined to get the last word in.

I was just on the verge of opening my mouth to cut him dead with a crushing retort when he took my hand and dragged me towards the lit-up dance-floor.

'Nat!' I hissed. 'Carter'll be looking for me.' I tried to loosen Nat's grip on me but he was having none of it.

'But it's *Horny Horny Horny*,' he protested. 'It's practically our song!'

Nat whirled me round like we were on *Strictly Come Dancing* and I had no choice but to give in.

That's the other thing I love about Nat, he's the only boy I know who'll dance with me without worrying that he's being girly or uncool.

I finally managed to disentangle myself from Nat. My feet were not happy. I was sure there were some blister-type things going on but I was more worried about Carter. I eventually found him slouched against a pillar looking like he was having the worst night of his life. My heart sank, I should never have forced him to come. I hobbled over to him, hoping he wasn't going to be too angry.

'Sorry, I bumped into Nat,' I began but he smiled and handed me my lukewarm drink.

'It's OK, Edie, you don't have to explain,' he shouted above the music. 'I like watching you dance, you really should think about going into cabaret.'

I could feel my cheeks flushing and I turned my head away from him. Carter gently took my chin in his hand so he could see my face.

'What do you want?' he enquired throatily.

'I don't know,' I said breathlessly. 'I want to sit down and I . . . I'm really hot.' Please kiss me, I silently begged him and I was just about to do something pathetic like plead with him to smooch me when Atsuko and Darby came over to say hello.

'We interrupting something?' asked Atsuko, sensing the atmosphere.

'Edie and I were having a moment,' Carter said, putting an arm round me and pulling me against him.

'Hi,' I managed to get out finally. 'I'm just having a bit of a hot flush.'

'Hmmm, you do look all weird,' commented Darby. 'Like you've been running a marathon.'

'I've been dancing with Nat,' I continued. 'Anyway I didn't think you two were coming. It's not really your scene, is it?'

'We didn't think you were coming either,' said Atsuko. 'We're only here to get a snog from every bloke we ever fancied in the two years we were at college.'

'And we're not leaving until we do,' finished Darby fiercely.

I could feel Carter tense up. 'I think I'd better get Edie out of here before you two give her any ideas,' he said smoothly. 'I hope you've brought some lip balm, it sounds like you're going to need it.'

I could tell that Atsuko and Darby weren't sure whether Carter was laughing with them or at them and to tell you the truth I wasn't either.

'Hey, rewind,' I said, flashing Carter a warning look. 'We've only just got here. I want to spend some time with my friends.'

Carter shrugged in a fairly good impression of

someone who was fine with that idea, but not before I saw the flash of annoyance that swept across his face.

'I'll go and see Matt then while you compare nail varnish or whatever it is you girls talk about,' and he walked off in the direction of the DJ booth where one of his friends was hanging out.

Atsuko and Darby visibly relaxed. 'I'm surprised he doesn't have you electronically tagged,' sniped Darby as we grabbed a booth.

'I can't believe I'm seeing a boy who all my mates loathe,' I said miserably. 'I know he can be sarcastic but he can be really sweet too. Honest.'

'Are you trying to convince us or yourself?' asked Darby as she took a sip of her lurid pink cocktail.

'I'm really confused about the way he makes me feel half the time,' I confessed. 'When he gets all toxic on me I end up wanting to kiss him.'

'Classic evasion tactic,' explained Atsuko whose dad's a psychologist. 'You think that if he kisses you, he'll stop being all arsey. Whereas he's being all arsey 'cause he knows it makes you uncomfortable and then he gets to be the one in control. Do you know what I mean?'

'No, not really,' I admitted.

'She means he's a complete control freak, Edie,' said Darby in an exasperated voice. 'You practically had to ask for his permission to spend time with us.'

'It's complicated,' I said, trying to explain. 'I had this mini-fling thing with my ex . . .'

'Dylan?'

'Yeah, well Carter's convinced that I'm the least trustworthy girl in the Manchester area 'cause I was kind of seeing him too,' I finished unhappily. 'You must think I'm a terrible person, like, boy-obsessed or something.'

'Everyone has boy issues,' said Darby consolingly. 'I once had three boys on the go 'cause I couldn't make up my mind which one I really fancied.'

'But you're with Carter now, right?' asked Atsuko. 'So he should get over it.'

I gave a deep sigh. 'But he refuses to acknowledge the fact that we're practically going steady. He just says that we should keep it loose but . . .'

'But?' prompted Atsuko.

'He reckons that if we are going out then we should, you know, um, have sex but I'm not sure,' I managed to stammer. 'It seems like a lousy reason. Right?'

'Right!' agreed Darby. 'It's one thing to have sex 'cause you're in a serious relationship with someone you care about. But to do it with someone in the hope that he might decide to actually admit that you're already having a relationship, well that's just twisted.'

'Edie, what are you doing with that guy?' Atsuko demanded.

'I don't know.' I fisted my hands in my hair. 'I know he can be difficult but it's exciting at the same time.'

'Boys can be such jerks,' said Darby feelingly.

There was a moment's silence as we all contemplated the jerkdom of the male species and I was pleased that I was bonding with them, even if it was over Carter's lack of boyfriendliness. I looked up to see the man himself looming over me.

'Edie, please can we go?' he begged. I looked at Atsuko and Darby. They were no help.

'See you at rehearsal tomorrow then,' they both chirped and slid out of the booth. 'Right, let's find our first victim,' Darby added.

'Good luck!' I called after them.

Which left just me and Carter. He ran a finger down my cheek, 'Let's get the hell out of here.'

We got a taxi back to my house and the minute I opened the front door I kicked my wedges off.

'Ow!' I whimpered. 'My feet are officially killing me.'

Carter laughed and followed me into the lounge. I made some tea and he dumped all the cushions off the settee and we sprawled out on the floor and listened to Belle and Sebastian. It's strange with the parents off the premises. Like, it's my house or something (although I would never have chosen such disgusting soft furnishings). To start with we drank our tea and didn't really say anything but this time the silence was companionable. When there aren't any other people around Carter completely chills out. He's funny and we talk about books and films and play 'anywhere but here'. And Carter strokes Pudding, my cat, until she's all purred out and I think I could really love him.

But then I don't want to go that deep with Carter 'cause on some level I know that the closer that I let him get, the more he'll be able to hurt me someday. Could my thought patterns be any more skewy?

An hour later I was stretched out on the carpet while Carter lay over me, his hands gently pinning my arms to my side while he nibbled at my bottom lip. It was frustrating not being able to touch him as his tongue sank into my mouth. He let go of my wrists and trailed a hand down my side until I felt him start to push the skirt of my dress further up my leg. I kind of blissed out as he tickled the underside of my knee but when his hand reached mid-thigh I tugged it away. Carter behaved himself for a while and concentrated on kissing me until I was gasping for breath but as he reached under me and started to inch my zip down, I sat up and pushed him away.

'No!' I yelped.

'No?' he asked, reaching for me again but I brushed his hands away. Carter got to his feet and gave me an annoyed look.

'I'm not going to wait forever, Edie,' he said. 'You have to lose it sometime, you might as well lose it with me.'

'It just doesn't feel right,' I tried to explain. 'I'm not ready, it's too soon.'

'Is it me?' Carter wanted to know. 'Are you scared?'

'I don't know. I suppose so. Sometimes I think you're only interested in me 'cause, you know, you want to . . .'

'God, you can't even say it,' said Carter sounding really exasperated. 'People have sex, it's no big deal.'

'Well, it is to me,' I muttered. 'I want it to be special. I want to lose my virginity with someone who lo— who really cares for me. I don't want my first time to be on the living room carpet.'

Carter shook his head. 'I've gotta go,' he said. 'I'll call you.'

I scrambled to my feet. 'Don't be mad at me,' I begged, trying to give him a hug. He gently but firmly held me off.

'I'll call you,' he repeated and was out of the front door before I could say another word.

22nd July

I didn't sleep at all last night. In fact, I spent most of the night tossing and turning and whacking at my pillows as I tried to get comfy. All I could think about was what Carter had said. Maybe he was right, maybe I was making a big fuss out of nothing. In fact, when I thought about it I realised that I was the only girl I knew who was still a virgin. Apart from Poppy's sister Grace and she's only fifteen or something.

It isn't like I'm worried that it's going to hurt (well not completely) but the longer I hold on to my virginity (I hate *that* word), the more difficult it is to think about actually bumping uglies with someone. And although Carter gets me all hot and bothered and occasionally I feel like I'm really into him, is he the person I want to have sex with? I mean everyone says you never forget your first time and fifty years from now do I really want to have memories of Carter going where no boy-shape had gone before? But what really bugs me is wondering whether I should have had sex with Dylan back when we were together or semi-together. Despite all the crap he's put me through, it would have been, I don't know, *fitting* for him to have been my first. I mean he was my first everything else. My first boyfriend. My first boy that I loved. The first person to break my heart into tiny little pieces and grind them into the ground with his heel. Or, then again, maybe not.

23rd July

I didn't sleep again last night! I think I'm going down with insomnia or something. I just get into bed and my head is whirling with A-level Fear and Boy-related Worries. All this nocturnal soul-searching leaves me sleep deprived and majorly crabby. This morning I finally managed to drag myself out of bed and into a cold shower which a) did nothing to make me feel more awake and b) left me feeling even more bad-tempered. I was actually kind of sorry that The Mothership wasn't around so I could unleash some of my aggression by snarling at her before I went to work.

I pulled on some boy-cut trousers and a faded, old T-shirt 'cause it made some crazy sense to look as horrible as I felt, shoved my still aching feet into trainers and scraped my hair back into a ponytail before stomping out of the front door.

Even though I'd managed to tut loudly at old women getting in my way and pulled faces at any un-suspecting small child who'd dared to even cross my line of vision I still felt hissy when I got to work. And there was Dylan looking all foxy even with a chef's jacket on and his faded jeans that hung low on his hips. He gave me a lazy wave and smile from the serving hatch (oh, the cheek of him!) which I ignored as I grabbed my order pad and a pencil and marched over to a couple of businessmen who were waiting to be served.

It wasn't my fault. When you're feeling icky and some stupid suit tells you to 'cheer up love, it might never happen' they're lucky that you don't chuck their breakfast special into their lap. Anna hurried over just as the fully-laden plate I was holding was beginning to tip lapwards and ordered me into the kitchen for the rest of the day.

I banged open the kitchen door and glared at Dylan and Italian Tony, the other chef.

Dylan nearly jumped out of his skin but Tony just laughed.

'I make you some black coffee, Edie,' he said with a twinkle. 'And you don't speak if you don't have anything nice to say, huh?'

I gave Tony a look, which just made him laugh as I opened a loaf of sliced white and attacked the first piece of bread with my butter knife. We worked in silence for an hour until Tony announced that he was off to the cash and carry and sauntered out.

'I leave you in charge, Edie,' he announced. 'But no picking on the new boy.'

The minute Tony was out of the door, I turned and glared at Dylan.

'You couldn't get a summer job somewhere else, could you?' I hissed at him. 'You have to find work where you can bug me for the next eight weeks.'

Dylan looked hurt but I was immune to his puppy-dog eyes these days. 'I've known Anna for ages. I have worked next door to her for three years,' he pointed out mildly.

'Why can't you work in Rhythm over the summer?' I demanded.

'Can you stop pointing that knife at me?' said Dylan nervously. 'They don't need any more full-time staff and I'm behind with my rent so Anna said I could help out here. Mind you, if I'd known you were going to be such charming company maybe I'd have started working here ages ago.'

'Oh, ha ha,' I said sarcastically. 'Anyway I didn't even know you could cook.'

Dylan looked incredibly uncomfortable and shifted his gaze to the griddle where two misshapen sausages were doing a good impersonation of charcoal.

Although I hadn't thought it possible I started to grin. 'Oh my God!' I yelped.

'Leave it!' said Dylan warningly.

I ignored him. 'You can't cook,' I crowed. 'You can't even make a decent cup of coffee! How did you think you were going to manage as a short order cook?'

'Are you going to carry on like this all day or are you going to help me?' asked Dylan with a bite to his voice as the sausages started to smoke.

'I guess you're on buttering and slicing duties,' I told Dylan as I gently pushed him out of the way and started to scrape the meaty mess off the griddle plate.

I guess Dylan was worried that I was going to 'fess his lack of culinary expertise to Anna, which I so wasn't but he tried to be really nice to me. In between making up the sandwiches for lunch he kept offering me endless cups of tea and muffins while all I could do was bitch about how I was going to stink of bacon fat and try to keep my eyes open. Sometimes it frightens me how much I enjoy behaving like a complete cow.

In the end Dylan abandoned his attempts to jolly me up. I think the final straw was when he asked me if I was going to any festivals this summer. 'We're not friends, Dylan,' I reminded him. 'Things are completely crap between us, which is entirely your fault, so stop pretending that you give a shit.'

I can be quite the badass when I haven't had my normal eight hours' worth of shut-eye.

24th July

Jesus, I've turned into one of those boring people who bangs on and on about their job, like, the whole time.

I managed not to speak to Dylan all morning because I was serving out front but the atmosphere between us was still slightly more frosty than the North Pole. I'm also still not sleeping (maybe it has something to do with being on my own in the house?) and it makes me so touchy. No wonder his continued presence makes everything that much worse. I have to admit I've also been worrying about Poppy spending quality time with Dylan. They know each other to say hello to but she's *my* friend.

I've worked really hard to make new friends that have nothing to do with my old friends and the thought of Dylan and Poppy even being in the same room for

128

any amount of time makes me feel queasy. Not least because she knows that it's hard for me to turn off my feelings for him, the kind of feelings that I've tried to bury really deep so no-one would know they were there.

But what the hell do I know? She came in to cover the lunchtime rush today and after ten minutes, the pair of them were acting like they'd been friends forever – it was enough to make me puke.

After lunch I went on my break and managed to grab an hour's snooze on some sacks of flour in the storeroom and when I surfaced I felt relatively human again.

I bounded back into the kitchen and peered into the fridge.

'I'm starving!' I announced to Dylan who was spooning mayonnaise into little bowls. 'Have we got any chicken left?'

'Oh hi Edie, your evil twin was looking for you earlier,' he said drily.

I pulled a face. 'I'm sorry,' I said in a small voice because I had been acting like a bitch on wheels. 'I didn't sleep very well last night.'

Dylan gave me an all-penetrating look. 'You don't look like you've slept well in ages. You've got huge dark shadows under your eyes.'

'Cheers for that, tact boy.'

'It makes you look all mysterious,' backtracked

Dylan fast. 'Like you've been staying up all night to write intense poetry.'

It was impossible to be mad at Dylan any longer. I just couldn't do it. 'Nothing that exotic,' I told him with a smile. 'I've just got a lot on my mind.' Like you and your girlfriend's brother, I added to myself.

But Dylan was nodding and making some sympathetic comment about my A-level results and how he knew I'd ace them.

I started making up the mixture for tomorrow's muffins and sang along with the radio while Dylan did the washing up. I looked up from my stirring to find him watching me with a sad little smile.

'What?' I asked defensively.

He shook his head. 'It's weird seeing you in work mode, that's all. I forget how capable you are.'

'You and Carter both have a vested interest in treating me like a little girl half the time,' I muttered darkly.

'Is he being his usual overbearing self?' asked Dylan with a cold edge to his voice.

I gulped. 'I don't want to talk about him.' There was a moment's silence before I continued. 'Anyway, yup, I'm a very capable girl, as my mum is always telling me, and I shall be taking over the world in approximately two years, three months and seventeen days.'

Dylan chuckled at that and made some sarky remark about me staging my first military coup before the end of summer.

We had such a good time this afternoon. We didn't mention Veronique or Carter, just pratted about and sang along to Dylan's iPod. And as I walked home I wished that it could be just me and Dylan again. Like how it was before but better 'cause I'd done loads of growing up since then and I really didn't know how I was going to get through the summer having to see him every day. Plus the weather's starting to get really hot and I'm probably going to die from chip fat inhalation.

27th July
Thank God for band rehearsals that save me from sinking into a big gloom about the thought of spending the summer in Manchester. I had a nap when I got in from work and a long L'Occitane Green Tea bubble bath-scented soak so I was feeling no pain. When I got to the rehearsal room that we've started to use, Atsuko and Darby were already there. And so was Grace, Poppy's really shy little sister.

'Hey,' I said as I knelt on the floor to open my guitar case. 'So, how many guys did you two pull the other night?' I added, as Atsuko plonked herself down on the amp next to me.

'Eight or nine,' was the casual reply. 'I lost count to tell you the truth.'

'Oooh that's so skeevy!' I shuddered. 'What about Darby?'

'She ended up copping off with that art boy she's fancied for the last six months,' groaned Atsuko. 'She's spent all week clutching her mobile and waiting for him to call.'

'Been there, done that, still working through the pain,' I muttered.

'So what did you and Carter get up to?' Atsuko asked.

I winced. 'Had a big argument about why I wouldn't shag him.'

'So the usual then?' laughed Atsuko.

'Yeah . . .'

'Are you two going to gossip all day or are we going to work on songs for our first platinum-selling album?' called Poppy from the stage where she'd been fiddling with her mike stand.

I think I'm turning into a rock chick on the quiet. Even though playing the guitar gives me backache and makes my fingers hurt, I'm really getting into throwing rock-god shapes as I actually make proper chords come out of my guitar. I even like singing (well, shouting if I'm being honest) on the choruses and doing harmonies while Poppy screams out lyrics about how crap boys are and how she's actually a trained assassin. I spent most of the rehearsal thrusting out my hips and brandishing my guitar or trying to jump off the drum riser and master A flat diminished at the same time. I never thought I'd say it but I wish I'd paid more attention during GCSE Music. No wonder I only got a C.

I also love hanging out with girls. It's not at all like hanging out with boys, for which I'm eternally grateful. It's weird but being forced to join this band by Poppy has turned me into the fourth member of a gang and her and Atsuko and Darby have become my best friends. I'd forgotten how cool it was to have girl buds. I'd never burp in front of Dylan or try and turn a Pringle over in my mouth while Carter was watching but I can do all those things with these girls and it just makes them like me more.

We finished the rehearsal with our killer tune, Fang Boys Suck, our homage to *Buffy the Vampire Slayer*. I'd just managed to complete my guitar solo without making any mistakes and was concentrating on shouting, 'Mr Pointy's coming to get you, fang boy!' at the top of my voice when I realised that Carter was leaning against a stack of broken amps by the door. I immediately hit a bum note earning me a glare from Poppy. And suddenly I thought, screw him! I was in a band. I had a job. I had a life away from him. He'd just have to deal with the real Edie instead of the embarrassed little girl I became when I was with him. I took that thought and ran with it or rather I stepped on to the drum riser for my final guitar flourish and jumped off as the song reached its noisy and dramatic final note.

There was a moment's silence while we tried to catch our collective breath and then it was broken by the sound of Carter clapping. Not a sardonic slow hand-clap but proper applause.

'That was fantastic,' he exclaimed as he walked towards us. I pulled off my guitar and looked at the others.

'We're not really ready for an audience,' Poppy said, but she couldn't stop herself. 'Did you really think we were good? 'Cause we don't want to be, like, a sad girly band but I think we kick ass in a tuneful way.'

'I thought you were brilliant. All of you,' said Carter with more enthusiasm than I'd ever heard him muster before. 'Edgy but commercial too. Like this old girl band called The Raincoats.'

'I *love* The Raincoats!' squeaked Poppy.

And I was like, Carter is actually being genuinely nice and well, unCarterish to one of my friends? Must be a full moon.

Carter looked at me. 'I never knew you could play so well,' he said quietly. 'You looked so cool.'

It was like Carter had been abducted by aliens. He helped us pack all our gear away in the rehearsal complex's storeroom and insisted on taking us to the pub to buy us a congratulatory round. Poppy sent Grace off home 'cause we'd never get served anywhere with such an obviously underage girl in tow, and we walked to the Dry Bar which was just around the corner. Carter even held my hand *in the street* and kept shooting me admiring glances and smiling at me. I guess I should have let him come to rehearsals more often.

Poppy loved him because he knew about all the obscure indie bands that she was into. Atsuko and Darby were warming to him because he was their 'in' to a world of foxy art boys and even I managed to forget what a pig he'd been the night of the college graduation party because he was squeezing my hand and generally acting like I was a princess among (sort of) girlfriends. It was a complete revelation.

I broke up all the mutual admiration that was wafting about at ten o'clock when I said that I was going.

'Oh, stay, Edie,' whined Poppy. 'It's early.'

'I've got to be at work by 8.30 all this week,' I reminded her. 'It's OK for you, you don't have to be in till lunchtime.'

'Oh, oh, no fair,' she continued to whimper as Darby's mobile rang and she ran outside to take the call.

'I smell art boy,' said Atsuko tartly as I stood up and pulled on my cardie.

'Well, I'll see you tomorrow,' I said to Poppy, 'And I'll see you two soon,' I said looking at Carter and Atsuko.

Carter was having none of it. 'You getting the bus home?'

I nodded. 'Yeah, it stops at the top of my road.'

He got up. 'I'll come with you. Well, I'll walk you to the bus stop.'

I ignored Atsuko and Poppy's raised eyebrows and smirks as Carter slung an arm round my shoulder and we walked out of the door.

Carter had made major concessions to actually behaving like a normal boyfriend but kissing in bus shelters was always going to be a step too far. He did hold my hand while we waited for the bus though.

'I suppose you're not going to let me come home with you?' he eventually asked with a half-smile.

'Hmmm, you suppose right,' I told him.

He gave me a mock punch on the chin. 'But you'll think about what I said the other night, won't you?'

I rolled my eyes. 'Look we've had a really nice evening, please don't ruin it.'

'I'm not,' he protested. 'I just know we'd be great together. I'd make it really good for you.'

'There's my bus,' I said gratefully as it lurched into view. I turned to him. 'Just give me some time, OK?'

He bent down and pressed his lips to the corner of my mouth. 'Make it soon, Edie.'

1st August

Life's kind of rearranged itself into a routine over the last week. I work and try to pretend that I can handle spending large chunks of time with Dylan. I rehearse with the band. And I wait for Carter to call. And wait.

And wait. I guess I could call him but I'm determined to win this round. So with all this working and longing and rehearsing and waiting, the days just seem to drift by.

2nd August

I so heart Sunday lie-ins. I was attempting to get out of bed in time to get to the local Farmers' Market to buy cake when my phone rang.

I groped for it on my bedside table, still stupid with sleep, but awake enough to feel a tiny flicker of hope. Maybe it was Carter. It wasn't. It was Shona who I haven't spoken to in forever.

'Edie? Is that you? Did I wake you up?'

'Yeah, you did actually,' I mumbled. 'But I was going to get up soon anyway.'

'Well it is one o'clock,' she pointed out. I could hear the irritation in her voice even down the phone line.

There was a moment's silence.

'So how have you been?' I finally asked but Shona wasn't in the mood for idle chatter.

'I need to talk to you,' she said abruptly. 'Can you meet me?'

'If it's about Dylan, then no,' I snapped. 'We just work together. That's all and we're, like, totally chaperoned all the time so if someone . . .'

'What the hell has Dylan got to do with anything?'

she asked. 'Or are you just doing a really crap job of covering up the fact that you two are *still* seeing each other?'

'We are NOT seeing each other!'

'OK, sorry,' she sighed. 'I'll meet you by the lake in . . . can you be ready in an hour?'

'Yeah,' I agreed in a resigned voice and hung up. I didn't know what Shona wanted but I knew it couldn't be good.

2nd August (later)

I felt sick as I walked towards the park. Shona had a real nerve. 'Cause if you think about it (and I have done quite a lot), Dylan and I would never have broken up in the first place if it hadn't been for the whole Mia business, which would never have happened if Shona and Paul had sorted out their own freaking mess, instead of getting Dylan to do it. I couldn't even remember the last time we'd hung out together, just the two of us. Which wasn't that surprising because you'd think her and Paul were conjoined twins or something, plus she so obviously prefers Veronique to me even though you'd have to be a complete mentalist to do that. That's my latest theory. That Dylan and Shona and their crowd are all addled in the head. Why else would anyone actually want to spend quality time with that witch?

Anyway, I digress. It was really hot, the sun was

glaring down and I was glad I'd smothered myself in sunblock before I left the house. It was way too hot to wear anything more than a loose cotton dress, definitely no man-made fibres.

Trying to put off the icky situation a bit longer, I stopped to buy an ice cream from the van at the park gates, but there was no escape, Shona was waiting for me by the bridge and I tried to casually stroll towards her like her phone call hadn't freaked the hell out of me.

'Hey,' she said pensively.

'Hey,' I replied through a mouthful of Mr Whippy. We walked around the lake and made polite conversation about the band and Shona's job at a web design company. This used to be the girl who I could talk about anything with and now we were having serious problems trying to sustain a five-minute conversation.

I couldn't bear it any longer.

'What's all this about, Shona?' I asked her. 'We haven't spoken in months so something must be wrong if you suddenly need to talk to me.'

Shona pulled a face. 'Let's get out of the sun.' Shona always reckons she has Eskimo blood in her veins. She is the whitest person I've ever seen, apart from, like, Goths, so I pointed to a bench under the shade of a willow tree.

'Let's go and sit down.'

I looked at her curiously as she sat down. Even

though it was easily ninety degrees, Shona was wearing a big baggy *jumper*. Obviously my mentalist theory had been bang on the money.

'Aren't you hot?' I said.

There was a pause. 'No . . .' The pause carried on for several millennia, while I tilted my head and waited expectantly, which was actually not a good choice of word because finally she blurted out: 'I'm pregnant.'

'What?' I hadn't been expecting that.

'I'm two weeks late, Edie, and I'm usually regular to, like, the minute,' Shona said bitterly.

'Oh,' I was stumped for what to say. 'So are you and Paul pleased?'

She gave me a furious look. 'Do I look pleased? I'm twenty, I've just started my career, I'm still living with my parents. I think it's safe to say that I'm not exactly jumping for joy.'

'I'm sorry,' I muttered. 'How did it happen?'

'How do you think it happened?'

I blushed. 'I know *how* it happened but I thought you were using some protection.'

Shona slumped on the bench. 'The condom split and I didn't have time to get any emergency contraception with work and stuff. I thought it would be all right.'

She looked so utterly miserable sat there that even though we'd stopped hanging out I put an arm around her. 'Shona, it'll be all right,' I said. 'Paul loves you to death . . .'

She twisted out of my hug. 'It won't be all right. He won't talk about it; he just pretends that it isn't happening. I can't talk to him about whether I'm going to have a termination or keep it or anything. He changes the subject.'

'Maybe you could talk to Dylan, get him to have a word with Paul,' I suggested nervously, not really wanting to mention the D word.

'I don't want to talk to Dylan about it . . . boy . . . girl stuff, urgh,' Shona tailed off. 'I wondered whether *you*'d talk to Paul.'

'Me?' I squeaked. 'Why me?'

' 'Cause you're a disinterested third party,' said Shona. 'And Paul's always liked you.'

Which was news to me because I only ever thought of Paul in terms of someone else. First he'd been Dylan's mate and then he'd been Shona's boyfriend. 'Well I've always liked him too but, God, I haven't spoken to him in months,' I pointed out. 'I wouldn't even know what to say to him.'

'Look, you just go round to their flat, pretend you need to see Carter or something and then mention that you've bumped into me and you're worried about me and you think—'

'You've thought this all out, haven't you?' I interrupted. 'You want me to go and tell your boyfriend that you're upset about, that . . . I mean, what do you actually think I could say to him that would make any difference?'

'I don't know,' snarled Shona. 'You think if I knew what to do I'd ever have phoned you?'

I could feel icy shivers tracing a path down my spine. 'What's that supposed to mean?' I asked.

'Well, Edie, you haven't really been much of a friend in the past have you?' said Shona. 'You treated Dylan like hell when you were going out with him, you tried to split up his relationship with Veronique even though you could see that they were happy and then you stop talking to me because I actually had the audacity to be friends with Dylan's girlfriend.'

It was like having a bucket of cold water thrown in my face. Yeah, those were the barest of bare facts but that wasn't really what had happened. I didn't even have the energy to argue with Shona. How could I explain to her why I'd done all the stupid, crazy things I had? And how could I tell her that Dylan had been more than agreeable when it came to sneaking around behind everyone's backs?

'You can think what you like,' I told her quietly. 'It's all history now and it's between Dylan and me anyway.'

'Oh, are you going to cry now, Edie?' taunted Shona. 'Isn't that what you usually do when it all gets too much?'

'Maybe I've changed,' I said. 'And maybe you have

too. Like, when did you become such a bitch? Look, I'm sorry that you were caught in the middle of me and Dylan and Veronique and I'm sorry that we don't talk any more and I'm sorry that you're pregnant but I'm not a bad person. I had my reasons for doing what I did.'

Shona looked at me like she was seeing me for the first time. 'You *have* changed,' she said slowly. 'You used to be really sweet.'

'I'm out of here,' I announced, standing up. 'You're going through stuff, I totally get that, but do whatever it is you have to do to deal and don't sodding well take it out on me.'

Shona caught hold of my wrist and tugged me back. 'I'm sorry. It just makes me sad. You used to be all innocent and sparkly. It's why I don't hang out with you these days 'cause you never really smile any more. It's like you're hiding behind this wall you've built up.'

Seemed like Shona still knew me a little too well. 'No I don't,' I denied desperately. 'I'm still me. I got messed over Dylan and it's taken me a while to get over it. And I do smile. I smile all the time, but you're just not around to see it these days.'

I should have asked Shona about pregnancy tests and if she'd seen a doctor but all I said was, 'So couldn't you have asked Veronique to talk to Paul? I mean, you guys hang out all the time.'

Shona pulled a face. 'I don't really want to talk

about Veronique with you but she can be a little tactless sometimes and her and Paul don't really get on.'

'OK,' I said. 'I'll go and see him but I'm not promising anything.' I didn't know why I was agreeing to this stupid plan but if you could have seen how hurt and defenceless Shona seemed, you'd have done the same thing.

3rd August

If I'd gone to meet Shona with a heavy heart yesterday, then the walk round to the lads' flat today was even worse. It was a crazy idea and no good could come of it, I thought as I rang on their doorbell. Shona had reckoned that Paul would be in on his own when she'd phoned earlier and thankfully she was right.

'Hi Edie, Carter's out,' he said when he saw me standing on the doorstep. 'Or did you come round to see Dylan? You didn't, did you?' he added uneasily.

I managed to smile. 'No, I came round to see you. Can I come in, I've even brought my own supply of Diet Coke?'

It took a while for Paul to find a glass and clear one of Dylan's art pieces off the sofa and for us to talk about the weather but eventually we were sitting down and I started to launch into my prepared speech. But as I started to stutter about bumping into Shona and how she seemed really depressed I could see Paul fidgeting and not really getting it, so I decided to just let him have it.

I told him that Shona was beside herself with worry and that he was being a complete wuss and if he really loved Shona he'd be supportive and if she did decide to have the baby he was proving that he'd be really crap Daddy material. It took me a good ten minutes but when I finally ran out of steam, Paul was looking very shamefaced.

'But she hasn't even done a pregnancy test,' was all he could think of to say.

'Well go and buy her one then,' I shouted. 'And get her a bunch of flowers while you're at it.'

He was already on his feet and scooping up his keys when Dylan suddenly walked in.

Paul and I whirled around and I guess we both looked guilty because Dylan said in a suspicious voice, 'What's going on?'

Paul shot me a warning glance. 'Edie was just passing and she needed to, um, well she'd been meaning to, well . . .'

'I was looking for Veronique!' I squeaked. Where the hell had that come from?

Dylan looked even more wary. 'And why would that be?'

I looked to Paul for some help but he shrugged helplessly. I turned back to Dylan. 'I needed to see her because I'm having a . . . barbecue!' He was never going to buy this. 'Yeah, I'm having a barbecue and I wondered whether she wanted to come!'

Dylan arched an eyebrow and my heart started pumping painfully fast. 'So you could have told me about it tomorrow at the café.'

Paul decided to give me some help as he disappeared out the door. 'You know what Edie's like, she gets an idea and she has to act on it.'

Dylan was still standing in the middle of the room. 'Hmmm, you always were impulsive,' he said softly. 'It used to keep me on my toes.'

The atmosphere had changed. Now Paul was gone, the air in the room seemed to sizzle in a way that had nothing to do with the heat of the day. Dylan was looking at me in a really sultry way that made me very aware of the thinness of my dress and my bare legs and the way my toes were peeking out of my clumpy Dr Scholls.

'So anyway I bumped into Shona and we hadn't really had a chat for ages,' I started burbling to fill the silence and because I still wasn't sure if Dylan was convinced by the whole Veronique invitation thing. 'And we decided it would be cool to have a barbecue and we should have it at my place 'cause, y'know, 'rents off the premises and then we thought it would be good if it was just girls and it would be a chance for me and Veronique to get to know each other . . .'

Dylan put a finger to my lips and I jumped back like he'd burnt me.

'What did you do that for?' I demanded in a wobbly voice.

'I thought you were going to pass out if you didn't stop to take a breath soon,' Dylan said huskily. 'You always talk too much when you get nervous. Am I making you nervous?'

'Of course not,' I said, though you could have heard my heart thudding in the next county. 'I should be going.'

Dylan and I hadn't really been alone in the same room since Veronique's ultimatum and now I knew why. 'Cause I couldn't trust myself with Dylan and I couldn't trust him either. Plus he was being all flirty, which usually led to us getting all kissy and then it was always me who had to deal with the fallout.

'Can't you stay for a drink?' Dylan asked pleadingly. 'It's too hot to go racing round the streets of Manchester.'

I dithered. 'Well, I don't . . .'

'Oh, c'mon Edie,' drawled Dylan. 'We have more Diet Coke in the fridge and ice cubes and a fan.'

Of course I stayed. Just call me Princess Pushover.

Dylan moved the fan so that we got blasts of delicious cold air wafting over us as we sat on the sofa. The breeze lifted Dylan's dark hair and I itched to stroke it. I stole surreptitious glances at him as the fan moulded his T-shirt to his lean body and his mouth wore a special half-smile that he always had when we talked.

And we did talk. Like the months we'd been apart had melted away to nothing. Even when Dylan and I talk about silly things like the dress I want to buy or the boys he works with in Rhythm Records, the conversation means so much more than the things we're actually talking about.

'You're not OK, are you, Edie?' Dylan suddenly said. 'I know there's something wrong.'

There were loads of things that were wrong like me angsting about my A-level results and my future and whether I should have sex with Carter but what was really bothering me was the chat I'd had with Shona the day before.

I picked at a tiny scab on my knee. 'It was something that Shona said,' I muttered. 'Do you think I've changed? Do you think I pretend to be someone that I'm not?'

I was curled up in one corner of the sofa while Dylan was sprawled over the remaining three-quarters. He shifted his long body so he was right against me, looking intently at my face.

'Everybody changes,' he said carefully.

'She said that I never smiled any more and that I used to be all sparkly and stuff,' I whispered. 'I s'pose she thinks I've turned into a hard-faced cow.'

Dylan reached out and stroked a loose tendril of hair back behind my ear and I was a good girl, I pretended to flinch away from him, even though he was now all busy with the wrong touching and the stroking of my cheek. 'I think if you've changed it's because you got hurt. And I know I was the one who hurt you and let you take the blame. We've never talked about it, have we?'

I tried to pull his hand away from my face but before I could let go he clasped my fingers in his.

'What's the point, Dylan?' I said with a sigh. 'You were with Veronique then, you're with her now. I knew what we were doing was wrong but I didn't do anything to stop it.'

'Neither did I,' Dylan reminded me gently. 'And I knew that Carter and Veronique were gunning for you and I just let it happen. Do you remember when Veronique and I came round to see you and she said all those horrible things and I just stood there and let her? I hated myself.'

'But I pursued you relentlessly,' I protested, but lamely, 'cause, quite frankly, my heart wasn't in it.

'And I could have made more of an effort to stop you but I didn't,' admitted Dylan fiercely, squeezing my hand tighter. 'And when Carter started coming on to you, the thought of him touching you made me so angry.'

'But it's all in the past now, isn't it?' I said. 'You're going out with Veronique and I'm going out with Carter. Sort of. Hey, it's kind of weird how stuff turns out, don't you think?'

'Look, I want you to know that I'm sorry I was such a bastard,' Dylan was saying when we heard a key turn in the lock and Carter talking on his phone. We both exchanged horrified looks.

'He'll kill me if he finds me here with you,' I hissed.

Before I could think straight Dylan was tugging me to my feet and pushing me down in the gap between the sofa and the wall.

'Stay there and don't make a sound,' he ordered quietly.

I shifted uncomfortably and pulled my knees up against my chest as I heard Carter come into the lounge.

'Oh, it's you,' he said to Dylan. 'I thought I heard voices.'

'I wasn't expecting you back,' Dylan managed to say casually.

'Forgot my credit card,' said Carter shortly. 'I'm going to go and see the lovely Edie. Got a problem with that?'

'Don't want to hear it, mate,' Dylan bit out.

'I think she's been missing me,' continued Carter smoothly. 'Which always makes her a little bit clingy. It's actually quite adorable.'

It was a little disconcerting to hear Carter talk about me. Like, he was taunting Dylan or something. I'll never figure him out if I live to be a hundred.

'Well if she does call,' Carter was saying, 'tell her I'll

be round in an hour and I can't wait to give her a great big kiss.'

Dylan snarled something very rude and I heard Carter chuckle as he left the room. I waited a few more seconds until the front door slammed and Dylan's head appeared over the back of the sofa.

'It's all right, he's gone.'

I managed to squeeze out of my hiding place (it had been much easier getting in there) and tried to stretch my legs. My calf muscles were protesting.

'I've got cramp.' I collapsed into an armchair. Dylan knelt down in front of me as I rubbed the back of my leg.

'So what was all that . . . what the hell . . . ?' I squealed as Dylan put one of my feet in his lap and started to gently stroke my tense muscles.

'Shush,' Dylan said firmly. 'I'm just making you feel better.'

The touch of his hands kneading out the knots was pure bliss. And when the knots had gone, Dylan carried on stroking my leg. All of a sudden I couldn't breathe. I looked at Dylan with confused eyes and he stared right back at me, almost daring me to make him stop, before bending his head to kiss my knee. I knew that all I had to do was reach forward slightly and Dylan and I would be on the floor, with our mouths locked together. By the glint in his eye I could tell that he knew it too. For a moment I did nothing and then

I was reaching forward but it was only to push Dylan away so I could stand up. 'I'm out of here,' I said decisively. 'We really shouldn't be alone together.'

Dylan groaned as he fell back on the floor. 'I can't even look at you without wanting to do things that I shouldn't.'

I couldn't help myself. 'What kind of things?'

Dylan gave another groan. 'Things that would make you blush if I told you about them.'

11th August

Paul has got the biggest mouth in the history of orthodontics. He only went and told Veronique about the barbecue and now I actually have to go ahead and have the bloody thing. I'm glad it's going to be girls only though, I can't cope with any more boy-induced tension.

The one good thing about last Sunday was that Shona and I have found our friendship again. She phoned today to tell me that Paul was making all the kind of noises that a decent boyfriend would in the same situation. She even apologised for all the mean things she'd said.

'It must be my hormones,' she said without a trace of humour.

'Don't even! It's way too soon to even think of using that as an excuse. Have you decided what to do yet?'

'Well I took the pregnancy test but it was hard to tell

whether it was positive or not,' said Shona. 'I mean I'm not ready to have a baby, I can barely look after myself.'

'Sex always ends up getting complicated,' I said feelingly.

Shona snorted in surprise, which wasn't a very nice sound to have in your ear. 'Have you? With Carter? Oh God, it wasn't Dylan, was it?'

'I haven't with anybody,' I said indignantly. 'But I'm thinking about it.' Carter had come round the night before and spent two hours alternating between kissing the stuffing out of me and getting really annoyed when I wouldn't let him go below the waist.

Shona tactfully changed the subject. 'So who's coming to this babes-only barbecue?'

'Atsuko, Darby and Poppy who I'm in the band with . . .' I started.

'I met them before,' Shona reminded me. 'And can we expect a little performance?'

'Hmmm, Poppy reckons we're going to do an acoustic set but we'll see about that,' I muttered. 'If Poppy's coming then her little sister Grace will come too but she never says anything to anyone. And I invited Nat 'cause he's an honorary girl and you invited Veronique for me, didn't you?'

'Yeah, I'm not sure if she's going to turn up though,' Shona said hesitantly. 'She really doesn't like you.'

'The feeling's mutual but it'll earn me some brownie points with her brother,' I added thoughtfully before I rang off.

Oh no, my life isn't at all complicated.

15th August

I'd got way too much food in. Anna let me clear out the fridge at work yesterday and everyone had chipped in a fiver anyway. The kitchen table was groaning with quiches and salads and crisps and cocktail sausages, which I'm usually addicted to, but it was so hot, I didn't feel like eating and Shona insisted that the smell of any kind of meat by-product made her feel sick.

I was just trying to fire up the barbecue when Poppy, Atsuko, Darby and Grace turned up. I waved at them and went back to reading the instructions on the self-lighting charcoal that our next-door neighbour had given me. It might just as well have been written in Urdu for all the sense it made. The doorbell rang and I could see that the others were preoccupied with making dramatic inroads into my ice supply so I hurried to answer it. Veronique was standing on the doorstep looking about as happy to see me as I was her.

'Hi,' she said distantly and tossed a stray lock of her bright red hair over her shoulder. It was *so* dyed. Why would anyone willingly choose to have hair that colour?

'Glad you could make it,' I simpered in my best hostess voice. The Mothership would have been so proud if she could have heard how polite and friendly I was being. 'You must be hot, let me get you a drink.'

Veronique stepped past me and gave me a look as if to say, what are you *on*? 'Where's Shona?' she asked rudely.

I pointed in the direction of the garden. 'She's out there, I think.'

'You've got some gooey stuff on your dress,' Veronique pointed out with a smirk as she sauntered past.

I looked down to see a huge glob of coleslaw on my new dress and with a sigh I ran up the stairs to change. I was just pulling on my shortest denim skirt and hunting round for a top when the doorbell rang again.

I practically fell down the stairs as I tried to pull on a top at the same time.

I was still buttoning up when I opened the door. I mean, it was only going to be Nat and he'd seen me in various states of undress whenever he slept over.

But it wasn't Nat. Paul, Dylan, Simon and Carter were standing there with a couple of the lads from Rhythm Records, clutching some bags from the off-licence and looking at my bare midriff. I clutched the gaping sides of my top together.

'Do you need a hand with the buttons?' enquired Simon with a wolfish smile while I just stared at them.

'You're not meant to be here,' I said eventually as they began to push past me.

'Don't worry about it,' said Carter comfortingly, leaning down to kiss my cheek. 'We're your official gatecrashers.'

'But I haven't got enough food,' I wailed as I followed them down the hall into the kitchen.

'Jeez, Edie, you've got enough food to feed the population of a small country,' Paul said with a laugh when he saw the buffet.

'I've got some barbecue-y stuff too,' I confessed. 'Not that I can light it. I s'pose if you're staying one of you can use your ancient fire-making skills.'

We went out to the garden and Veronique immediately got up from her deckchair to curl herself around Dylan who'd barely glanced at me since I opened the door. Shona seemed to know everyone and Poppy knew Will and Robbie 'cause they came into the café every day for their lunch while Atsuko and Darby were looking decidedly chipper at the presence of boy-shapes. So much for spending quality time with the sisterhood, I thought. Everyone was introducing themselves, apart from Grace who, as usual, was fidgeting on the sidelines.

I touched her arm. 'D'you want to help me light the barbecue?' I asked her gently. She nodded.

The self-lighting charcoal still wouldn't. Grace watched silently while I lit match after match and swore as I tried to get the stuff to ignite.

'You could try chucking some lighter fuel on it,' suggested Carter coming up behind me and placing a kiss on the back of my neck. He definitely improved when there was company present.

'There will be no chucking and no lighter fuel,' I said firmly as he took the matches out of my hands and lit the charcoal on his first attempt.

I clapped my hands. 'I'm impressed. You've obviously got hidden talents.'

Carter gave me a smouldering look. 'You have no idea,' he said softly.

'We're not talking about barbecues any more, are we?' I teased him.

Grace exited fairly sharpish as Carter nudged me with his hip. 'Nope,' he said, pulling me towards him for another kiss.

He always does this. He seems to know when I've had enough of him and turns up being so sweet and affectionate that I forgive him for all his past sins.

'So, do you want me to use my ancient fire-making skills to cook meat as well?' demanded Carter. 'It might take my mind off the fact that you've still got four buttons undone on your top.'

Although my plans for a boy-shape-free zone had been ruined, the barbecue was actually a success. Once Nat had turned up and everyone had pretended to eat and given up because it was too hot, a game of girls versus boys footie had started. After we'd trounced them five goals to two and had collapsed on the grass while Poppy ordered Grace (who hadn't played) to make us some drinks, I found myself sitting next to Veronique. I thought she'd have been all snooty about doing something as uncool as playing six-a-side footie but she'd been the girl of the match, scoring three of our goals. 'You were really good,' I told her. 'I couldn't believe the way you tackled Will like that.'

She grinned at me. 'I'm quite skilful when it comes to getting rid of the opposition but then you'd know all about that, wouldn't you, dear?'

I didn't know how she could sit in my back garden, drinking my wine and have the nerve to say something like that. She wasn't talking about football. Oh no. She was talking about me and Dylan and doing it when no-one else was around so she could keep her sweet girl rep. I tried to count to ten and not have a major hissy fit but I'd only got to five when I saw Poppy bearing down on me with my acoustic guitar.

'It's too hot,' I told her before she could even open her mouth. 'My fingers are way too sweaty to play.'

'I'm not taking no for an answer,' Poppy said, blithely ignoring my pained face. 'Everyone's dying to hear us.'

'No they're not,' I argued. But Shona who was sitting nearby gave me an evil smile and cooed, 'Are you going to do that acoustic set that I've been looking forward to all day?'

Poppy hauled me to my feet, still protesting, and shoved the guitar at me. 'You strum, I'll sing and Atsuko and Darby are going to improvise.'

Accompanied by Darby on a tambourine that she'd pulled out of her backpack and with Atsuko on harmonies, we did a couple of our own songs which sounded weird, quite frankly, without the full-on shouty treatment before launching into our version of Rihanna's 'Rude Boy'.

When we'd finished I caught Dylan's eye, he was staring at me with such longing that it made me catch my breath. It was only when Simon asked if we were going to take any requests and Poppy dug me none too gently in the ribs that the moment passed.

'I can't play that many things,' I insisted when Will and Robbie pleaded with us to play something by Tinie Tempah. 'I can do some Beatles and that's about it.'

Any oldster stumbling into the back garden would have been delighted that young people could still make their own entertainment as we spent the next half hour singing along to Beatles songs and forgetting most of the words.

By the time my strumming hand had started to cramp up, it was getting dark. It was still swelteringly hot, so I lit little Chinese lanterns to keep the midges away and switched on my fairy lights, which I'd draped over the trelliswork before everyone had arrived. Our garden had been transformed into a fairy grotto. I lay back on the grass contentedly and listened to the conversation washing over me. It was so nice when everybody forgot all the reasons why they hated each other and just chilled out. Even Carter and Dylan seemed to be having a civil conversation about the Surrealist Movement. Art boys, eh?

I wasn't the only one inspired by all this group bonding as I heard Simon suddenly exclaim, 'We should all go to a festival before summer's out.'

I rolled my eyes. The day I went to a festival and slept in a tent without the benefit of my summer-weight duvet was the day they buried me. No-one else seemed to share my opinion though. There were enthusiastic noises of agreement from all sides and I could have voiced my dissent but knowing how flaky my guests were I reckoned that any mass outings were never going to happen. I smirked as Will mentioned that a record company sales rep had offered him some cheap tickets to a festival in Devon then frowned as Poppy added that Anna would probably let us borrow the café's van. This was starting to sound suspiciously like a plan. I was just about to point out all the pitfalls of sharing a field with a bunch of tree-hugging hippies when Atsuko plonked herself down next to me.

'D'you wanna know a secret?' she giggled.

'Yeah!'

'I think Simon's really cute,' she whispered. 'He's just asked me if I want to go to a gig with him tomorrow.'

'Cool,' I said. 'Simon's a sweetie.'

'You should know,' came Veronique's voice from somewhere behind me. 'She got off with him,' she added for Atsuko's benefit.

I sat up and glared at her. 'Who told you that?'

Veronique held my gaze. 'Carter told me. It wasn't a secret, was it?'

I was going to kill Carter. Once in a moment of weakness I'd told him that I'd snogged Simon. And I only told him because we were having an intimate moment and it seemed like a good idea to be honest with each other. My mistake.

I jumped to my feet as Shona came over to investigate the raised voices. 'It was a one-off,' I told Atsuko, who was looking at me with a hurt expression. 'We'd both had too much to drink . . .'

But Veronique wasn't finished. 'In fact, the only boy she hasn't made a play for seems to be Paul,' she remarked to Shona conversationally. 'I'd keep your eyes on him, if I were you.'

'That's not funny, Veronique,' hissed Shona as I tried to count to ten again. It was no use. I was going to whack Veronique if I stayed in the garden. She was just standing there, a satisfied smile on her face. With a frustrated groan I took a step towards her but Atsuko grabbed my arm and dragged me into the kitchen. The strip light made my eyes hurt as Atsuko pulled me towards the sink and told me to splash cold water on my face.

'I kissed him once,' I repeated. ' 'Cause I was upset and I was trying to make Dylan jealous. It was a hideous mistake. We don't even talk about it . . .'

Atsuko held up a hand. 'OK, just calm down,' she said soothingly. 'It kinda freaked me out for a minute that you'd snogged him but it's all right.'

'Really?'

'Look, I'm not that naïve,' Atsuko said with a smile. 'Simon seems like a bit of a player but I can work with that. Obviously he's been with other girls, I just didn't realise you were one of them.'

'I wasn't with him,' I protested. 'It was just a kiss.'

'I know,' said Atsuko. 'Please don't start getting hysterical. Go upstairs and put on some more mascara, you've washed yours all off. And I'm going to go and ask Simon if you're a good snog. Joke!'

'Oh, ha ha,' I said sourly but I followed orders and walked slowly upstairs. I didn't re-apply my Maybelline Wonderlash but I sat on my bed with my head in my hands. 'Sometimes I just want to disappear and never come back.'

I must have said it out loud 'cause I heard Dylan's voice from the doorway saying, 'I don't know what I'd do if you left.'

'You'd manage,' I told him, looking up and in that split second that our eyes collided, it was almost as if I was back in his living room because the tension was there again and the only thing that was preventing us from kissing was our own willpower. Which seemed to be in very short supply.

I held out my arms as Dylan practically stumbled towards me and then we fell back on my bed, his body covering every inch of me, our lips searching and then finding. All my nerve endings were so over-sensitised that when Dylan kissed my neck I whimpered because it felt so good even though it felt totally wrong too. I tried to pull him back to me as he suddenly shifted away from me. But he was only pulling his T-shirt over his head and throwing it on the floor before settling back in my arms. He planted little kisses along the way as he undid each button on my top and our legs tangled with each other, as my skirt rode up.

The last fragment of my rational mind registered the irony of the situation. Like, Carter had been badgering me for weeks and all I could do was come up with excuses about it not being the right time or the right place and now I was with Dylan and the door was wide open and anyone could burst in on us and I didn't care. All I cared about was the scrape of Dylan's teeth on my tongue and the frantic drumming of his heart against my chest and the chaos his fingers were causing as he stroked my back.

'Make me stop,' Dylan groaned, making no effort to pull away from me.

'I don't want you to stop,' I whispered and Dylan caught my mouth again in a hard, frantic kiss. His hand curled into the waistband of my skirt and nothing was going to stop . . .

'Edie. Um, Edie . . .'

There it was again, that nagging little voice that must have been my conscience.

'Edie!'

Dylan paused. 'Did you hear something?' Was my conscience *that* loud? I tried to get into the kissing and the thundering towards losing my virginity again but the moment was gone. Especially when I glimpsed Grace standing at the doorway looking like she was about to burst into tears and bleating, 'Edie! Edie!' at me.

In one movement I pushed Dylan away and jack-knifed off the bed.

'How long have you been there?' I yelled at her, once again grabbing the sides of my top and folding my arms.

'I was calling you but you, er, didn't hear me,' she whispered in the tiniest voice I'd ever heard.

'I'm sorry I shouted at you,' I said, trying to catch my breath. And I was like, my God, she actually speaks. Dylan, with T-shirt back on, stepped in front of me to shield me from her curious gaze. Grace's eyes were popping out as she looked at him, then me, then back to Dylan again.

'You never saw this,' he said to her sharply. 'Edie and I we're just . . . we got carried away.' He could say that again.

'People are going now,' Grace said. 'They wondered where you were.' She gave us another incredulous look and scampered out.

'You'd better go downstairs,' I said, moving away from him to put as much space between us as possible. 'Say I was being sick or something. The heat . . .'

'Is damage limitation all you can think about?' Dylan demanded. 'Don't you think we should talk about what just happened?'

'It was stupid what just happened!' I said fiercely. But it hadn't been stupid. It had been glorious and wonderful and thrilling. And must never happen again. I walked out of the room without looking back.

It was obvious that everyone was wondering where Dylan and I had disappeared to but I cobbled together some silly story about the heat and eating too many cocktail sausages and vomiting and when Dylan appeared he and Veronique left immediately. The others followed. Shona and Paul stayed behind to help me clear up and finally they went too but Shona was back to being weird with me. *Quelle surprise.*

I went out into the garden and sank down on the

sunlounger. I felt lousy. I was a bad, bad person. I wasn't to be trusted, especially with other people's boyfriends. But Dylan was more than someone else's boyfriend. No matter how hard we tried to be apart from each other, some force that I couldn't even begin to explain drew us together. Like magnets or something.

'It went rather well, don't you think?'

I gave a start as Carter walked towards me.

'I thought everyone had gone home,' I muttered.

'No, I'm still here,' he said softly. 'I made you a cup of tea. I heard that you got sick.'

I moved my legs so he could sit on the side of the lounger and took the mug from him. It was dark but I could see the searching look he gave me. And I *knew* that he knew what Dylan and I had been doing. I just did. And Carter might have been difficult and high-maintenance but he didn't deserve the treatment he was getting from me.

'What are you thinking?' he asked.

My mouth twisted. 'I was wondering why you put up with me.'

Carter reached out to stroke my hair back from my face. 'Maybe I think you're worth the effort.'

It was all very well breaking my heart over Dylan but it was always doomed to failure. Whereas Carter was right here, right now. He wasn't going anywhere, he was staying with me, despite all the grief I gave him.

'Carter?'

'What's the matter, honey?' he asked, nestling me into his arms.

'I've been thinking.' I took a deep breath. 'I *will* sleep with you. Not tonight but very soon, I promise.'

21st August

I read this interview with Madonna once and she said if you wanted something badly enough the whole world would conspire to make sure you got it. Much! I want to go to this pikey festival as much as I want to be locked in a room with Veronique but at every turn I'm thwarted. I don't want to sleep in a tent or have communal showers or be forced to eat veggie burgers injected with large doses of salmonella and I've heard awful stories about the toilet facilities at festivals. But every time I say anything about not wanting to go, the girls call me a princess. And not in a good way.

Even Carter, a man famed for the sharpness of his suits and the volume of his quiff, seems uncharacteristically up for roughing it.

At least, I thought, Anna wouldn't give me, Poppy *and* Dylan the weekend off but she's decided to close the café for the bank holiday anyway and she's even letting us borrow her van. The same van whose back doors fly open if you take a corner too fast.

The parents are my last hope. They do this three times a week phone call thing to make sure I haven't killed the cat, the plants or myself. Yes, in that order. I'm sure they'll absolutely forbid me to leave the house unattended for four days.

But I'm not talking to them until tomorrow. AKA THE DAY I GET MY RESULTS! Oh God, I think I'm going to be sick. I'd almost managed to forget about my exams but really I've just been kidding myself.

I did do a lot of revision but that was in between severe bouts of boy-related mopeyness and I totally screwed up my French grammar paper. I'm doomed with added bits of doominess.

22nd August

She might be on another continental shelf but my mum can still really piss me off! I was quite happy to wait for my results to arrive in the post but, no, she had to leave strict instructions with Anna. When I got to work this morning she was standing at the door with the van keys in her hand.

'Hey Anna,' I said brightly. 'Shall I put the kettle on?'

'Nice try, kiddo,' was Anna's reply. 'In the van, I'm taking you to get your results.'

I whimpered something about planning to go in my break but Anna took my arm in a freakishly strong grip, for such a little woman, and practically lifted me onto the passenger seat.

We didn't say much on the way to the college. Anna asked me once if I was nervous and I lied and said I wasn't but when we went over a speedbump I thought I was going to puke. Anna took her *loco parentis* role far too seriously for my liking. She frogmarched me into college, obviously expecting me to bolt, and hauled me over to the noticeboard where the results were pinned up.

I stood there and gazed at a spot just above her head.

'Do you want me to . . . ?'

I shook my head. 'No, I'll do it.'

I tried to look at the board and everything was blurry. I traced a finger down the list until I came to the Ws and found, 'Wheeler, Edith'. I shut my eyes. This was my last moment of ignorance or irresponsibility. After this, I was either going to go to McDonald's and fill in an application form or actually commit to spending another three years of my life in an educational establishment. I heard Anna make an impatient clucking sound behind me and I opened my eyes and forced myself to look.

'What did you get?' asked Anna with a fair bit of exasperation.

'A star for History, an A for French, B for Psychology and an A star for English,' I managed to say before I burst into tears.

I'd been so good at pretending not to be worried about my results. I'd assumed an air of nonchalance for weeks while secretly angsting about them and while

I felt relieved I was also really sad too. Like, now I was set on the path of being a grown-up and having to make big decisions that were going to change my life forever. No wonder I was crying. But Anna was hugging me and then Atsuko and Darby were there and Atsuko had straight A-starred everything and Darby hadn't done as bad as she'd thought.

We were just about to make our getaway when I saw the college principal bearing down on me. He must have spent the last two years thinking I was a complete thicko because he kept going on and on about how surprised and impressed the faculty were with my results and what was I going to do about university? I muttered something about deferring and having a gap year and, besides, my parents were away and I didn't want to make any life-changing decisions. And then he said that I might even have a chance at Oxbridge and I just turned to Anna and said, 'Can we please go now?'

Well, I guess I'm not quite done with the book learning after all.

By the time I spoke to Mum and Dad – they'd stayed up all night waiting for me to call – when we got back to the café, I could have asked them for a pet elephant and they'd have agreed to build a jumbo kennel in the back garden. After Mum had finished cooing and Dad had got on the phone to say, 'Oh yes, quite good Edie, really,' which is what he comes out with when he's very impressed, there wasn't much time to say anything else. What I really wanted to say was that I was scared and confused and I wished they'd come home and did they think it was a good idea to have sex with Carter? But Mum insisted that I go to the festival as long as our neighbours agreed to feed the cat and then badgered me for five minutes about what I was going to do in my gap year. Apparently my options didn't seem to include moping around the house watching daytime television, which was all that I really wanted to do.

Once I got off the phone, Anna made me close my eyes and when I opened them Italian Tony was holding a cake in the shape of a guitar, which said, 'Congratulations'.

'I'd have had to change it to "Commiserations" if you'd failed,' he joked and then him and Anna started singing 'For She's A Jolly Good Fellow' and all the customers joined in. It was too embarrassing for words. But I couldn't be an ungrateful bitch so I smiled until my jaw muscles ached and acted like I was really pleased. Don't get me wrong, I was touched that Anna and Tony had gone to so much trouble but I just wished everyone would shut up about my sodding results and my bloody future.

Dylan had called in sick for, like, the third time this week, which I was eternally grateful for. We'd had an unspoken pact since the barbecue to studiously ignore each other but when Poppy came in at lunchtime she was studiously ignoring me too. Every time I smiled at her or caught her eye as we waited tables, she looked away. I didn't know what was going on with her. The minute that Anna put the sign to 'closed' Poppy was out of the door. I gave Anna a big hug for being an ace surrogate mum and raced after Poppy.

'Poppy! Wait up!' I called but she carried on walking.

I finally caught up with her at the bottom of the road. 'Didn't you hear me calling?'

She gave me a nervous look. 'No.'

'What's up?' I demanded, turning her to face me. 'You've been strange with me all day. Have I done something to piss you off?'

Poppy ran a hand through her messy blonde curls. 'I've been trying to plan out what I was going to say to you but everything I rehearsed sounded wrong,' she began.

'What are you talking about?' I asked in a confused voice.

Poppy took my hand and led me over to someone's garden wall and sat down next to me.

She sighed deeply. 'Carter made a pass at me last night.'

'What?!' I hadn't been expecting that and yeah, yeah, *yeah* I was shocked.

'I bumped into him in the beer garden of The Elephant's Head and we were talking about bands we liked and then some insect thingy landed on my shoulder and bit me. And he . . . Carter, I mean, he pulled me forward to see the sting and then he kissed my shoulder and before I knew what he was doing, he'd kissed me properly, on the mouth.'

'Are you sure?' I wasn't entirely convinced that I wanted to know the answer.

'Yeah, Edie, I'm sure,' said Poppy sadly. 'I told him to cut it out and he just laughed and said that I'd been flirting with him. But I hadn't. I just liked him, was all. He was someone to talk about music with.'

I tried to smile as if the whole thing was a silly misunderstanding. 'He probably had too much to drink . . .'

Poppy shook her head. 'He hadn't. And he said . . . no, it doesn't matter.'

'Tell me!'

'He said he was fed up with you playing games,' Poppy continued unhappily. 'And that he'd fancied me for ages and you were just seeing him to make Dylan jealous.'

I could feel the sun beating down on my back through my T-shirt as I sat there and listened to Poppy's confession. And as I looked at the tears trickling down Poppy's face I knew she wasn't lying. I might be able to snog someone else's boyfriend but Poppy was straight-edge, she'd never break the girl code. That didn't mean I wanted to believe her though.

'Are you sure?' I asked her again.

'I'm positive,' she said firmly. 'I didn't want to tell you but Atsuko and Darby said you'd want to know.'

'Christ, Poppy,' I exclaimed angrily. 'How many other people have you told?' I hated myself for that little outburst, Carter was the one I should be mad at, not Poppy.

'Just them and erm, Shona,' came the worried reply. 'I had to tell someone and Carter stomped off once I'd yelled at him and I bumped into her in the loo and she could tell I was upset about something.'

'No wonder you've been weird with me all day,' I said. I could have told her what I'd really been doing with Dylan in my bedroom at the barbecue 'cause it would have made her feel better but for some reason I didn't. I think it's called self-preservation.

'Are you and me all right?' Poppy asked.

'Oh, come here,' I told her and gave her a hug and made her promise not to worry about it any more.

As I walked home I tried to work out how I felt about Poppy's revelation. I was sorry that she was upset but I didn't feel any of the blinding white jealousy I felt when I thought of Veronique and Dylan together. Maybe it was because Poppy was my mate. And maybe it was because I knew that Carter must have been drunk. He'd been so patient with me, stuck by me while I prevaricated and tried to make up my mind. He wouldn't just bail on me like that, and not with a friend of mine. Carter wasn't stupid. He must have known that Poppy would tell me. Which made me think that he must have been really drunk. I mean, why else would he have done it?

It had been such a tempestuous day, I must have gone through every emotion invented. The last straw was the next-door neighbours agreeing to look after Pudding while I was stuck in a field with the kind of people I normally cross over the road to avoid. I couldn't understand why Fate was being such a meanie. The neighbours normally spend most of their time complaining about Pudding because she keeps having sex with tomcats while everyone's trying to sleep. God, even my cat was doing it!

When I finally got indoors, I felt so restless – I didn't know what to do with myself. It was beyond hot and I was so confused about every single last bloody bit of my stupid, little life. I threw my clothes off, pulled on my new boy-cut bikini bottoms and bandeau top, and started filling my old paddling pool. With the 'rents away our household was using hardly any water so I felt I could safely flout the hosepipe ban. Finally I was at peace, sitting in five inches of cold water with a tub of Ben & Jerry's Cookie Dough ice cream. The summer wasn't going to get much better than this.

Or worse, I thought as I saw Carter climbing over the garden gate. I was just about to scramble out of the pool but thought better of it. There was no elegant way to get out. Although I was slightly thrown because I hadn't planned on having it out with him while I was half-naked in a kiddies' paddling pool.

'I tried ringing the doorbell but there was no reply,' he said sauntering towards me. 'You look . . .' he paused for effect, '. . . quite enchanting.'

I tugged my top more securely into place and folded my arms as Carter squatted down by the pool next to me.

'So did you get your results?' he asked after a minute had gone by and I hadn't said anything.

'Yup,' I said shortly.

'And they were good, bad, indifferent?' he prompted.

'They were fine,' I hissed.

Carter took off his shades and gave me an annoyed look, narrowing his dark blue eyes and curling the top lip of his beautifully sculptured mouth. He looked like he'd been carved out of marble. 'What's up with you?'

'What's up with me?' I couldn't believe his nerve. 'I had a chat with Poppy today,' I spat out. 'She told me that you . . . you . . . that you tried to get off with her last night!'

Carter froze for a second before going completely ballistic. He said I was a selfish little bitch who'd spent the last few months putting him through hell. He said that Poppy had been drunk and made a pass at him. And he said that I'd strung him along for ages and he'd just taken it like a fool. And finally he accused me of using Poppy's story as an excuse not to have sex with him. I had to sit there in the paddling pool and listen while Carter shouted at me and hurled a couple of deckchairs down the length of the garden in his fury.

'OK, I'm just going to walk out of here now,' he said finally. 'Then I'll be out of your life for good. It'll save you having to come up with sad stories like this. I love you but obviously that's not enough for you.'

As he turned to go I realised that he must have been telling the truth. Why else would he have got so mad and been so hurt? Or offered to leave when he'd spent months hanging around waiting for me to get over Dylan? And although I didn't think that Poppy had lied, maybe Carter was right and she'd been the one who was drunk and couldn't remember what had really happened. Besides, he *loved* me! He was the second non-family person in the world to ever say that they loved me.

'Carter, don't go,' I pleaded, standing up. 'I'm sorry.'

Carter carried on walking.

'Please come back,' I begged, starting to cry. 'I've said I'm sorry.'

He turned round slowly, looking shamefaced. 'Oh, don't cry,' he said huskily, walking back to me and pulling me into his arms. It felt so good to be held by someone. I wound my arms round his waist and clung on for dear life and sobbed all over the Fifties bowling shirt, which was his pride and joy.

Carter made soothing noises and stroked my hair. 'There, there, baby,' he purred. 'I'm not going anywhere.'

'I'm sorry,' I repeated. 'I had to believe Poppy.'

'I know you did, sweetheart,' Carter said soothingly. 'But do you really think I'd have hung around this long if I'd been jonesing after another girl?'

'I guess not,' I choked out.

And then Carter suddenly swung me up in his arms, climbed into the paddling pool and settled down with me on his lap.

'You're mad,' I said, laughing even though I was still crying a bit. 'All your clothes are wet.'

Carter shrugged. 'They'll dry.'

Our faces were so close I could see the tiny scar that almost touched the top of his lip. I stroked it with the tip of one finger.

I was sitting in my flowery pink bikini on the lap of a fully-clad boy in a paddling pool and it felt normal. And really, really nice.

I pulled Carter's head towards me and kissed the corner of his mouth gently. He smiled at me.

'Aren't you going to kiss me properly?' he said. 'You've never had any trouble before.'

I kissed him again and his lips parted to let me snake my tongue into his mouth. I liked being the kisser and not the kissee for once. I kissed Carter harder and tugged at him so we were both lying in the water with our entwined legs dangling over the edge. Feeling better, I started unbuttoning his shirt and Carter's hands which had been idly caressing my back stilled.

'Don't you want to?' I whispered. 'I was going to make it up to you.'

'That sounds interesting,' Carter drawled. 'How were you going to do that?'

'I thought we could, y'know . . .' I ran my hand down his chest in what I hoped was a suggestive manner.

'Are you saying what I think you're saying?' Carter asked, a hint of a smile playing at his lips.

'I think I'm ready,' I said decisively. 'Yes! Let's do it.'

Carter held my face in his hands and gave me a long, deep kiss before getting to his feet and reaching out a hand to me. I let him pull me up.

He placed his hands on my shoulders and looked me in the eye. 'I'm going to pass this time, Edie.'

I tried to twist away from him but he held me tight. 'Oh thanks for letting me make a complete idiot of myself,' I said bitterly. 'I thought it was what you wanted.'

Carter tucked my hair back behind my ears and gave me a gooey look. 'It is,' he insisted. 'And I'm incredibly tempted but I want you to have sex with me when it's right for you. Not because we've had a row and you want to make it up to me. Trust me, I know what I'm saying.'

'I feel so stupid,' I muttered, still standing in front of him.

'Well you shouldn't,' he said firmly. 'It was generous and lovely of you and you'll never know how much I want to take you upstairs and ravish you to within an inch of your life.'

'Yeah, right.' But I was smiling. It might have taken some time but what I was feeling towards Carter now was definitely a love thing.

'Are you going to stick around?' I asked him as we walked back into the house hand in hand.

'You bet,' he answered giving me another marshmallow look and I knew he was talking about the months ahead and not just the next few hours. 'Why don't you put some clothes on before I change my mind and then we'll . . . what do you want to do?'

'Eat some food, watch some DVDs, make out a lot,' I decided. 'You interested?'

Then I ran up the stairs and jumped up and down on my bed because I was so happy I thought my heart was going to burst into millions of sparkly pieces.

25th August

The last few days have been so blissful on the Carter front. Almost as if we had an unspoken agreement to put all the bad stuff behind us and start our relationship again. No more lies, no more playing games with each other, no more listening to other people telling us that we're bad for each other. Which they did. Like, with knobs on.

I'd had a really horrible evening at rehearsal when I'd had to tell Poppy that I was still with Carter. She'd looked at me as if I'd just spewed green ectoplasm out of my stomach.

'But how can you, Edie?' she'd kept asking me. 'After what happened with him and me?'

'We cleared all that up,' I'd said. 'And even if it was true, I don't care 'cause it's brought us closer together.'

'What do you mean *if* it was true?' Darby had chimed in. 'Do you think Poppy would lie about something like that?'

Then Darby, Poppy and Atsuko spent the rest of the rehearsal muttering about toxic boys, and girls who were too dumb to see through them. I think they were trying to tell me something but, quite frankly, I didn't want to hear it.

Of course, Dylan could immediately sniff out that my life had suddenly got really good and wanted to do everything in his power to spoil it. He spent the entire week trying to corner me in the café kitchen and telling me that we had to talk but I can't be bothered to go through a painful post-mortem on our hopeless attempts to be friends. It always ends up with us snogging. But now I'm finally happy with Carter, I don't need to find comfort in Dylan's arms. I mean, it isn't fair on Dylan or on Carter. And now that I've made the decision to be with Carter, properly, I feel more relaxed than I've been in ages. I haven't actually told Carter about what happened between me and Dylan at the barbecue – I mean, there didn't seem to be much point. Not when things are going so well. What he didn't know, he couldn't get huffy about.

The only other blot on my otherwise blemish-free landscape is the thought of going to the pigging festival and Shona, who's still pregnant, still not sure what to do about it, and taking her frustrations out on me.

'Could you be any more in denial?' she'd said contemptuously when she'd heard on the vine that Carter and I had been seen engaged in a passionate PDA in the Odeon foyer.

'He's bad news, Edie. How can you not see it?'

'That was before,' I insisted. 'I think he comes out with those snarky comments because really he's shy.'

Shona just snorted and pointed out that if any other girl had tried that kind of remark in my hearing I'd have had her for breakfast.

All these negative remarks are making me even

more determined *not* to go to the festival. I just want to be shot of my virginity. I think Carter and I should just stay in Manchester and er, *consummate* our relationship away from the disapproving comments of our so-called friends. But Carter has this romantic notion that my first time should be underneath the stars amid lots of grass and probably some slug-type creepy crawlies as well. And so here I am sitting on my bed with a backpack on the floor and a bunch of condoms in my bag, getting ready to spend many, many hours in the café van as we drive to the festival. Ho hum.

25th August (later)
I'm writing this under cover of my sleeping bag (oh my God, I can't believe I'm *in* a sleeping bag), illuminated by a dicky flashlight, which is why my handwriting is doing strange fandangos all over the page.

The journey here was a total disaster. Honestly. The first thing was Veronique and Dylan having the mother of all arguments. I mean, it had a plot and a subplot and several walk-on parts and I'm beginning to realise what all that cryptic speak was about earlier this year when he nearly split up with her.

They were the last to arrive as we packed our gear into the van outside the café. Dylan's battered little Mini roared up and he'd uncurled himself from the driver's seat and stood there tapping his feet impatiently while Veronique scrambled over to his side of the car to get out. (It's been nearly two years and he still hasn't got his passenger door fixed.)

'Thanks for helping me,' she snarled at him. 'Get my stuff out of your stinking car.'

I looked at Carter but he didn't seem to find anything particularly wrong and carried on hauling bags into the van.

'Get it yourself,' Dylan was saying between gritted teeth but he got her gear out of the boot anyway. As he gathered the bags in one hand so he could slam the boot shut with the other, he dropped a small vanity case which burst open, spilling out all of Veronique's pots and potions and make-up.

If I thought Carter had gone ballistic in the garden the other day, it was nothing on Veronique's reaction when she saw her Clinique compact get run over. She was like a creature possessed. She flew at Dylan, slapping him and screaming obscenities at the top of her voice. That was freaky in the extreme, but what was even freakier was other people's reactions. Me and Poppy, Grace, Atsuko, Darby and the Rhythm Records boys all looked horrified but Shona and Paul just rolled their eyes while Simon muttered, 'Here we go again,' under his breath.

Dylan was trying to hold Veronique off without actually hurting her and kept on telling her to calm down but she seemed to get more and more worked up.

'You make me sick. I hate you,' she screeched.

Dylan eventually managed to push her away and keep her at arm's length.

'I don't need this,' he said quietly but forcefully. 'Just stop it.' Veronique went still for a moment and he finally let go of her and started to head towards the rest of us.

Then Veronique went for him again. 'Don't you dare walk away from me!' she shouted, her hand raised to slap Dylan round the face when Carter was suddenly in front of her and tugging at her arm.

'Come on, Ronnie,' he said in that voice he used with me when I was being completely unreasonable. 'Let's go for a walk.'

They disappeared down the street and Dylan let out a deep breath, his shoulders drooping.

'She's been a complete 'mare ever since she got up,' he muttered at Shona who rushed over to see if he was all right. The rest of us were still standing there gawping. The sight of Dylan standing surrounded by his friends, who were all trying to console him, but looking utterly alone really got to me. When I thought about it, he was the one that didn't smile any more. Not properly. Not with that smirk and raised eyebrow that had used to make me come over all unnecessary. But I told myself it was useless to think of Dylan as anything other than an acquaintance, I was with Carter now. And eventually the sight of Dylan and the way his jeans always hung low on his hips and the way his chocolate-brown hair always begged for me to tousle it wouldn't affect me any more. I just had to wean myself off him.

So anyway, we didn't exactly set off in the best of spirits and things went steadily downhill.

Poppy insisted that she wasn't going to sit in the back of the van, giving me and Carter a pointed look, and squeezed up front with Shona and Paul, who was driving. Oh, and Grace, who seemed to be more surgically welded to her sister's side than ever before, wedged herself between Poppy and the door. Atsuko declined Simon's attempts to persuade her to sit on his lap so she wouldn't keep banging herself on bags every time Paul changed lanes, while Darby was happily ensconced between Will and Robbie, and Dylan and Veronique were sitting away from everybody else (well as far away as you can get in the back of a dilapidated Transit van) looking like they'd just had a ferocious row. Which, actually, yeah!

The atmosphere in the van just got worse and worse. We argued about what music we were going to listen to, which service station to stop at and who got to sit next to the open window and we'd only been driving for an hour.

'We could play "I went to the festival" . . .' I suggested brightly, only to have my idea shot down with varying degrees of savagery. Dylan just gave me a filthy look and I knew he was remembering the time we'd gone to Paris and spent practically the whole journey saying stuff, like, 'I went to the festival and I took articles of clothing belonging to Paul Daniels, brine shrimp . . .' Those had been happier days.

Carter wrapped his arms tighter around my waist. 'Well, *I* thought it was a good idea,' he whispered in my ear. 'I can't wait to get you alone in a tent.'

Although I kissed his cheek and smiled at him, I wondered why the thought of losing my virginity with the boy I was really into made me feel like I was about to go into hospital for open-heart surgery.

Dylan had been watching me and Carter with narrowed eyes when all of a sudden he turned to the still-fuming Veronique and stroked her cheek lightly.

'I'm sorry, Ronnie,' I could hear him say. 'It was my fault. I should have remembered to set the alarm clock.'

Veronique gave him a look that would have turned weaker men to stone and shifted half an inch away from him.

'Oh, come on,' Dylan continued softly. 'I'll do anything to make it up to you.'

Veronique began to look interested. 'Anything?' she enquired with that cat-like smile I hated so much.

'Anything you want,' Dylan promised.

'Hmmm, what about that new pair of shoes we saw in Office?' she said. 'The snakeskin ones with the pink trim.'

'I'll buy them as soon as we get back,' Dylan said and Veronique gave a little cry of happiness and flung herself at him. I looked at Dylan with contempt. Since when did he get so sappy? Whenever he'd been on the business-end of one of *my* hissy fits, he'd just smirked and teased me out of it. I could have doubled the contents of my wardrobe if I'd just been a bit more of a princess. As Veronique was planting little kisses over every bit of Dylan that she could reach, he caught my eye and then deliberately captured Veronique's mouth in a long, passionate kiss.

'Hey you two, go book a room,' said Will, loudly.

They came up for air and I turned my head away but not before I'd seen Veronique throw a satisfied glance at Carter who continued to squeeze me tightly. It was like my own private version of hell.

After we'd been travelling for three hours and I was thinking if I had to listen to Will's iPod and *The Best Trance Album In The World . . . Ever* one more time I was going to rip my ears off, Paul stopped the van.

As he opened the big, sliding door and let us out I could see that we weren't in a service station car park about to pig-out on fast food. Instead we had stopped in a small village, complete with cricket pitch and duck pond and coachloads of American tourists, who were looking at us as if we'd just landed from Mars.

'Where's the nearest Caffè Nero?' Darby asked on behalf of us all but Paul and Shona just grinned.

'There's a little tea shop on the other side of the duck pond,' Shona said. 'But first we thought we'd take in the sheep-throwing contest?'

'There's a what with who and huh?' I asked in a very blonde way.

'Yeah, we saw a sign,' Paul grinned. 'Sheep-throwing! Had to check it out.'

What happened next was the freakiest thing yet. Grace stamped on Paul's foot, yelled something about cruelty to animals and stormed off in the direction of a nearby field/paddock type arrangement where there was bunting and crowds and other things that suggested that sheep were being thrown. Poppy ran after Grace, and Atsuko and Darby ran after Poppy, Paul hopped up and down and made over-the-top 'ow' grimaces and I collapsed on the ground and laughed and laughed at the look on his face. Carter gave me an amused glance and told me to get up but by then I was curled in a ball with tears streaming down my face.

'Paul's face . . .' I kept trying to say while Paul flushed and grumbled that it wasn't *that* funny.

'Actually it was, honey,' insisted Shona. 'I never thought I'd hear that little pixie speak, let alone inflict GBH.'

'Dylan!' barked Veronique, sounding less than impressed. 'I'm getting a hunger headache, can we find something to eat in this godforsaken hellhole?' And she flounced off in the direction of a Ye Olde Tea Shoppe.

'Anything you say, sweetness,' Dylan bit out as he followed her, earning him a sharp glare from Carter.

'C'mon, Edieson Lighthouse,' said Shona pulling me to my feet. And it had been so long since she used her pet name for me (something to do with an old hippy band called Edison Lighthouse) that even though Carter was making 'let's slope off' motions at me, I linked arms with Shona and went off to investigate the sheep-throwing.

Grace had staged a one-woman protest by the time we got there and was being recorded for posterity on the tourists' camcorders.

'You're cruel!' she was shouting at some hapless farmer who had a distressed sheep on the end of a lead.

'Grace, you're upsetting the animals,' Poppy said, trying to calm her down. 'They're not really throwing the sheep. Are you?' she added anxiously at a tweedy-looking bloke who seemed to be in charge.

'My dear, it's more of a sheep jumping event. There are no sheep being thrown,' he insisted. 'It's all under the supervision of the local vet. We've been holding this tournament for over 300 years and I've never . . .'

'See Grace, nothing to get excited about,' I said

soothingly. 'Sheep like jumping. I'm sure I've seen some sheep-jumping videos on YouTube.'

Grace looked at me questioningly. 'Do you really think so?'

'Yes,' I said, managing to keep a straight face. 'Can we please go and get something to eat now, preferably nothing sheep-related?'

'Oh, OK,' Grace conceded, taking the hand I held out towards her. 'But if I find out you've been throwing sheep I'm reporting you to the RSPCA,' she hissed at Mr Tweed, before I could drag her away.

Once we'd tried to fill up on cucumber sarnies from Ye Olde Tea Shoppe and watched to make sure that the sheep weren't being thrown, it was time to get back in the van, which had heated up to furnace-like temperatures.

It wasn't too long before tempers were getting frayed again. Veronique and Dylan had had another row while we'd been doing the sheep thing so they were snarling at each other, Shona kept sniping at Will who'd produced some egg 'n' mayo sandwiches from his backpack 'cause the smell was making her feel sick and Atsuko and Darby had had a blazing domestic about whether Simon Cowell was gay.

I was fed up with the whole bloody lot of them. Carter had been stroppy ever since I'd gone off with Shona and I was seriously contemplating jumping out at the next pit-stop and hitching home. Instead I dug my iPod out of my bag, put my earbuds in and tuned the whole moaning lot of them out with a very loud dose of Florence & the Machine.

When we finally got back on the motorway, the van gave a dramatic splutter and got slower and slower before it shuddered to a halt. Luckily Paul managed to steer it onto the hard shoulder before it died altogether but we had to wait four hours in the burning afternoon sun for the breakdown vehicle to arrive. The only highlight of the wait, apart from everyone shouting at everybody else, was when Simon flagged down a passing ice-cream van and persuaded the driver to sell us some cold drinks.

It was six in the evening before we got started again and when we reached the festival site two hours later no-one was talking to anyone else, mainly because they'd fallen asleep, and we were stuck in a huge tailback that led to the main entrance.

Although I hadn't minded everyone not talking because it was less stressful than all the bitching, I knew I couldn't stay in the van one minute longer. To tell you the truth I was still vaguely thinking about doing a runner and hitching a lift to the nearest train station but even I could tell that was a *baaaaad* idea. I grabbed my backpack and my shoulder bag and crawled over to the door.

'I'm getting out,' I announced. 'I'll meet you at the campsite. I'm going to walk.'

People began to stir. 'But Edie, you hate walking,' Darby pointed out.

'And you'll get lost,' stated Carter with absolute certainty.

'No I won't,' I said crossly. 'We've already decided where we're going to pitch the tents. I've got a map and if I have to spend one more second in this van I'm going to kill someone. Probably Will.'

'What have *I* done?' asked Will indignantly.

'It's not you, it's your trance playlists,' I said.

'I never thought I'd say this,' piped up Veronique, 'but I have to agree with her on that one.'

My bolt for freedom didn't exactly go to plan. After ten more minutes of pointless arguing, we *all* left Paul and Shona to stay with the van and started walking towards the site. We walked and walked and walked until my feet were slipping around sweatily in my trainers. And Lord knows when I'd next get to have a bath. Not anytime soon that was for sure.

It was pitch dark by this time, lit only by the odd campfire, and we kept tripping over people until we reached the place where we *thought* we had decided earlier to set up camp. It was hard to tell. Of course, all the tent gear was in the van so we had to wait ages for Paul and Shona who'd parked somewhere completely different. It was 1.30 in the morning before we even *began* to assemble the tents, which led to more sniping and swearing as we fell over tent posts and got told off by the hippies in the next-door tent. Eventually all the tents were pitched. The only thing between me and an uncomfortable night in a sleeping bag was the decision about who was going to sleep where.

Carter had been all right up till now. Thankfully he'd slept for the last bit of the journey and woken up in a good mood, which lasted long enough for him to carry my bags up a big hill for me. I might be a feminist but I have no upper body strength. He was now eyeing up a little two-man tent and then eyeing me up and you didn't have to be a numbers geek to do the maths. The last thing on my mind though was getting naked and horizontal with Carter, I just wanted to sleep.

It was at that moment that Shona shunted Carter out of the way and got into the little tent. 'Me and Paul are sleeping in here,' she ordered in her don't-mess-with-me voice. 'Dylan and Veronique are sleeping in the green tent and then the two big tents are girls only and boys only. Goodnight.'

Carter looked annoyed so I tried to look annoyed too.

'Never mind, eh?' I said, kissing him on the cheek. 'I'll see you later.'

He grabbed me around the waist before I could walk off and pulled me tight against him. 'Tomorrow. We'll find some peace and quiet tomorrow, I promise.' But it didn't sound like a promise, it sounded like a threat.

I don't know when I'm going to get another chance to write. As it is, Darby and Poppy keep waking up and moaning at me for daring to rustle paper. Serves me right for still kicking it old skool on the diary front.

I'll probably do a big catch-up when we get back to Manchester. Jesus, I wish I had a time machine so I could jet propel myself home and it would already be several days from now.

31st August

Back home, thank the Lord. I'm typing this and sticking it in my diary because there's so much to say. Also, as God is my witness, I am never going to another festival as long as I live. That's an Edie promise. Anyway:

26th August

The festival was every bit as vile as I thought it would be. There were loads of beered-up lads wearing those ridiculous velvet jesters' hats with the bells on so at least you could hear them as they sneaked up behind you and tried to cop a feel. But even they weren't as bad as the masses of hippies in the healing field who were walking around bare-ass naked and ensuring that I'd never be able to eat another cocktail sausage as long as I lived. After a breakfast (well, lunch if we're going to get technical about it) of fresh doughnuts from a nearby stall, everyone split up and I was left alone with Carter. The girls had gone off to the fair and although they'd begged me to go with them, Carter had kept a tight grip on my hand and made it plain that we wanted to spend some quality time with each other.

We started walking down to the main stage and I forgot how nervous I was about what we'd planned to do once we were at the festival. He was just Carter, he wasn't scary. In fact, we spent the next half hour bonding as we moaned about the medieval bathing facilities and the annoying hippy brats that kept banging into our legs at five-minute intervals. Why is it little kids have no spatial awareness?

Carter and I sat and watched a couple of bands and I thought, this is good, this is what normal couples at a festival do, as we sat on the grass, holding hands and sipping lukewarm lager.

In between sets, Carter turned to me and took off his shades. 'I don't know how you do it,' he said, musingly.

'Do what?'

'You've had hardly any sleep, I know you're dying for a shower 'cause you've told me about ten times, but you look fantastic, like you've just stepped out of a Fellini film.'

I didn't actually know who Fellini was (though I

guessed he was some hip foreign film director) but I pulled a face. I did not look fantastic, not by anyone's standards. I had on a crumpled T-shirt and a pair of pink pedal-pushers that were already covered in grass stains. And however much sun-block I smeared on my face my freckles were multiplying by the minute. I tugged my fingers through my tangled hair.

'It's nice of you to say it, Carter,' I began. 'But I look and feel horrible. I don't know how *you* manage to stay so smart.'

It was true. Carter didn't have a single crease in his ensemble of checked shirt and dark blue jeans. He must have slept standing up.

Carter smirked. 'I'd be quite keen on getting a bit more rumpled.'

Here we go. I raised my eyebrows at him and he chuckled.

'Let's go back to the tent,' he murmured seductively. 'And I'll show you what you've been missing.'

I didn't say anything for a while. The tension hummed in the air between us and I knew that Carter was holding his breath. I couldn't put it off for any longer.

'OK,' I agreed with a sigh. He grinned and pulled me to my feet.

'You don't know how long I've waited to hear

you say that,' breathed Carter, leaning in to kiss me.

It had taken us half an hour to get to the main stage but with Carter tugging at my hand we made it back to the tent in ten minutes.

I stood there feeling completely detached, almost as if I was outside of myself, while he unzipped the canvas.

Carter held the tent flap open for me as I crawled inside, he was already unbuttoning his shirt as he inched towards me. This is it, I thought, I'm about to have sex in a tent, in the middle of a field, in broad daylight. It was not how I'd imagined this moment to be. Carter reached for me and pulled me down so I was lying on top of him and started to kiss me. His hands were stroking under my T-shirt as he whispered, 'You've got too many clothes on.'

I wriggled out of my T-shirt and wished this was happening to someone else as Carter began to fumble with the clasp on my bra. His eyes were roaming all over me and his hands weren't gentle as he twisted at the fastening. There wasn't a whole lot of tenderness going on. But how could I tell Carter that I'd made a mistake when I'd promised him I'd finally do the deed? There wasn't any going back . . .

Carter had managed to get my bra undone and was trying to coax me to slip it off when we heard a scuffling noise outside the tent. I froze.

'What was that?' I hissed as Carter rolled me over so he was pinning me to the ground.

'What was what?' he said impatiently.

'I heard a noise,' I said. There was another scrabble at the tent canvas. 'There it is again!'

The next second, to my horror, Poppy's head appeared through the flap.

'Oh my God!' we both squeaked. Poppy's head retreated and I grabbed my discarded T-shirt and held it to my chest.

Carter, God rot him, started to laugh. 'Foiled again,' he said, lying back with his arms behind his head.

I turned my back on him, did up my bra and pulled on my T-shirt before crawling out of the tent. And colour me puce 'cause every inch of me was blushing.

'I'm so sorry,' Poppy gabbled. 'I had no idea.'

'It's all right,' I muttered. I actually wanted to get down on my knees and kiss her feet in gratitude but I managed to restrain myself. 'What's up?'

She pulled me away from the tents. 'I don't want to be anywhere near *him*,' she said scathingly and then I remembered what *he'd* been doing the last time she saw him and winced.

'Forget him for a minute,' I advised her, wishing I could do the same. 'And tell me why you're so upset.'

Poppy gave a little cry of frustration. 'Grace has gone missing. I turned my back for a second and she's disappeared.'

'OK, where were you?' I asked, my Miss Efficiency autopilot kicking in.

'I was in the dance tent,' Poppy wailed. 'But I've looked all over. And the others are all looking and we can't find her anywhere.'

'All right, we'll get Carter to stay here in case she comes back and we'll go and look for her,' I decided. 'We've all got our phones and we haven't had time to run down our batteries. We'll find her.'

'Wow, Edie, I never knew you were so sensible,' Poppy exclaimed as I poked my head through the tent flap. Carter was lounging back on a rolled-up sleeping bag and grinned when he saw me.

'Ah, there you are,' he said wolfishly. 'I was beginning to think you'd abandoned me.'

'There's been a change of plan,' I said quickly, as he gave me an annoyed look. 'Grace has gone missing, Poppy's in a complete state and I need you to stay here in case she turns up. All right?'

'But Edie . . .' he started to say as I waved at him vaguely and turned back to Poppy.

'You go to the Missing Persons tent and I'll check

the animal welfare stalls,' I told her as we began to hurry down the hill.

'Thanks, Edie,' Poppy said. 'I don't know what I'd do without you. I can't seem to think straight.'

'You're just worried about Grace,' I panted as we picked up speed.

'Well, it kinda goes with the territory of being a bossy older sister. And, y'know, I'm sorry I've been so off with you,' said Poppy.

'Forget it,' I said and meant it. 'But please don't tell anyone about me and Carter . . . how we . . . what we were doing when you saw us.'

'Why would I tell anyone about *that*?' Poppy shrieked. 'It's scarred me for life!'

I checked the animal rights stalls and went back to the healing field but I couldn't find Grace anywhere. I bumped into Will and Robbie but they'd had no luck either. I was just about to call it a day and head back to find the others when I thought I saw Grace in the crowd. I pushed through people to get closer but she'd gone. I looked around helplessly and then I saw her. She was with a group of lads. They were all staggering about and laughing, Grace included, but she looked pale and confused. One of the bigger lads slung his arm round her and the pair of them looked like they were about to topple over.

I rushed towards her and Grace threw her arms round me. 'Edie! Lovely Edie,' she gasped. 'You look all weird.'

Her pupils were massively dilated and she was all floppy as if her limbs were made of Plasticine.

I turned to the lads who were standing there giggling feebly. 'What have you done to her?' I shouted. There was no response, just more giggles.

I poked the one nearest to me. 'What has she taken?' I demanded, grabbing the front of his T-shirt.

'Just some stuff,' he mumbled. 'I'll let you have a tab for a fiver.'

'What is wrong with you?' I yelled. 'Has she taken an E?'

'It was probably acid,' suggested this quite, quite beautiful boy who was part of the crowd that had gathered to watch. 'You wouldn't spike someone with E, it's too expensive.'

'Oh, OK,' I said distractedly but, like, not before I'd managed to clock how amazing-looking he was. I turned back to Grace, trying to keep her upright with one arm while I still had a grip on the boy's T-shirt with the other. 'You're lucky it was me who found you,' I snarled at him. 'If it had been her sister or one of our boyfriends, you'd be lucky to still have kneecaps.' I gave him a hard push and he fell over on the ground, still laughing at some private joke. I glared at his mates but they were just gazing at me like I should have come with subtitles or something.

'Hey! Hey! Listen to me! What have you taken?' I demanded of Grace, but she had her head nuzzled into my shoulder. There was drool going on too.

I shook her a teeny tiny bit and she finally came up for air. 'They bought me some water,' she said dazedly. 'And it made me feel all funny.'

'Do you need some help?' asked the beautiful hippy boy who told me his name was Azure as he gently took hold of Grace's other arm so we could get her to the First Aid tent. He was so stunning that in more normal circumstances I'd have been fighting for breath and losing myself in his amazing turquoise eyes, but I sternly told myself to stop it. This was not the time or the place. And besides Grace was babbling about how much she loved me and how some people looked like they had animal spirits inside them and she was beginning to seriously freak me out.

Azure disappeared once we got to the First Aid tent, after telling me that if I ever needed his services I could find him on the astral plane. The paramedics looked Grace over, told me that she'd probably taken some acid and the best thing I could do was sit quietly with her and make sure she drank plenty of fluid. Of course, then I realised I'd left my mobile in the tent so I had to fill in a form to get the DJ on the main stage to make an announcement so the others knew where to find us. Have I mentioned that I'm never going to another festival as long as I live?

Once the medics were sure that Grace hadn't ODd and wasn't about to go completely bonkers, they led us to a little Portakabin with a bed in it and I persuaded Grace to lie down. I sat there with her head on my lap while I stroked her hair and half-listened to her non-stop chattering.

Grace was all sunburnt and the curly blonde hair that looked all rock chick on Poppy, just looked like a bird's nest on Grace. I'd never noticed it before but she was actually very pretty. Much prettier than Poppy – though don't quote me on that. Grace was all soft and creamy, like the angels in my Renaissance art book. Yeah, she was very Botticelli. But she had to do something with her hair, possibly involving some intensive conditioning treatment and she also had to stop hiding her face behind her hands all the time. I s'pose it was hard having a sister like Poppy. Poppy was so determined and cool that any little siblings were forced to flail helplessly in her wake.

Anyway, Grace started trying to kiss my hands. I tugged them away gently.

'I'm so glad you're here, Edie,' she said, trying to focus her eyes on me. 'You're my friend, too, not just Poppy's. I wish you were my *best* friend.'

'Of course I'm your friend,' I patted her hand in what I hoped was a consoling manner. 'Why don't you try and get some sleep?'

'When I close my eyes I see this satanic version of Donald Duck's nephews,' she informed me solemnly. 'I wish I could remember their names.'

'Huey, Dewey and Louie,' I supplied.

Grace gave a chuckle. 'You know everything.'

I laughed. 'Remind me to come and see you next time I need my ego boosted,' I said.

But then Grace clutched my hands tightly and started saying how she wanted to be just like me and have boys fighting over her. 'You're my girl hero,' she insisted, getting more and more distressed.

'Please calm down,' I begged her. She looked at me all hurt. 'I'm not girl-hero material,' I told her bitterly. 'My life's a complete mess. I'm meant to be making all these big decisions about my future but I can't even decide what I want to do tomorrow. And I don't have boys fighting over me. I just have Carter and, y'know, he's, well he's *Carter*!'

Grace was silent after my outburst and I thought she'd dozed off but all of a sudden she opened her eyes and hit me with the question from hell. 'So why did you snog Dylan?' she asked baldly.

'Me and Dylan?' I whimpered. 'That's a whole other story.'

But Grace wanted to hear it and so I told her. Everything. All the gory, post-watershed details. All the stupid ways we'd managed to hurt each other. And why it was now over. When I finally got to the end, which must have been about an hour after I started, Grace looked at me with the steadiest of gazes and said, 'Why are you with Carter when you're still so in love with Dylan?'

I started trying to deny it but Grace interrupted: 'I hate Carter,' she announced dreamily. 'He tried to kiss me at your barbecue. After I'd seen you and Dylan and I was coming down the stairs and he was coming up the stairs and he pressed me against the wall and said he'd give me a go when I got a bit older. And then he kissed me and I didn't do anything because I knew that if he went upstairs he'd find you and Dylan.'

'Oh Grace, I'm so sorry.' I had this strange urge to wrap her up in the biggest blanket I could find and hide her away from all the shitty things in the world. I also had a less strange urge to find Carter and kick him right in the place where he did most of his thinking. Grace might have been on Planet Acid but it was obvious she wasn't lying. And

Poppy hadn't got her version of events wrong either. It sounded exactly like Carter, I could even hear his voice in my head drawling out the line about waiting till Grace was older. I felt sick at the thought of what I'd been prepared to do to keep him. He must have been laughing himself stupid at me for months. He was an evil bastard. An evil, lying, two-faced bastard.

'I wish my first kiss had been different,' mused Grace.

'They get better,' I promised. 'When Dylan kisses me it feels like, like I have this itch that only he can scratch but way, way, way better than that.'

Grace smiled and promptly fell asleep and I sat there going over my life since Carter had arrived to screw it up. I also tried not to think about whether I was still in love with Dylan like Grace reckoned. But what did she know? She'd just managed to get spiked, she wasn't exactly first in the queue when they were handing out great big bags of common sense, was she? By the time Poppy, Will and Robbie arrived, I was sunk into a big, bad gloom.

When I started to explain what had happened to Grace, Poppy burst into tears. Then Grace woke up and started crying too. I was severely tempted to join them. Once she'd calmed down, Poppy was so sweet to Grace. It was quite a sight to behold. I thought she might have given her a lecture about no-good boys and accepting drinks from them but she was more concerned that Grace was OK. I wished then that I had a big sister. I might not be in the mess I'm in now if I did. While I sat there cuddling Grace and Poppy, Will found a paramedic to give Grace another check. The medic reckoned that she just needed to sleep and that she might be a bit shaky tomorrow and then Will (his super-hero tendencies kicking in) picked Grace up and Robbie put his arm round Poppy and I trailed along behind them as we went back to the tents.

All I wanted to do was go home, crawl into bed (preferably one with freshly-washed sheets on) and stay there till the 'rents got home. While everyone was fussing over Grace I snuck into my tent and looked for the site-map to see how I could get home using public transport. I heard the tent flap open and steeled myself for a confrontation with Carter. I whirled around but it was Shona.

'Oh, it's you!' I said and then realised how that sounded. 'I didn't mean that the way it came out.'

'Glad to hear it,' she said reproachfully. 'Well you're a little heroine on the quiet, aren't you? I guess Poppy's forgiven you for the Cartergate incident.'

I shuddered. 'Don't talk to me about him. He's as good as dead.'

Shona raised her eyebrows, opened her mouth to say something and then thought better of it.

'Sorry, didn't mean to take it out on you,' I mumbled. 'I bet you're fed up with me and my psycho-dramas.'

'Hey, what are friends for,' Shona said lightly. 'So what I actually came to tell you was that I've just spent a fiver on a box of Tampax. Rip off, much.'

I goggled at her. 'So you're not . . . ?'

She bounded over and hugged me. 'Yay! My period's come! I'm not pregnant,' she crowed.

'Oh, I'm so pleased for you,' I said, wondering if that was the right thing to say. 'You're happy, right?'

'Ecstatic but I wish I wasn't surfing the crimson wave at a festival with primitive toilet facilities,' said Shona pulling a face.

'I hear you.'

'So what has Carter done now?' Shona asked.

'Oh I don't want to talk about it,' I groaned. 'Put it this way, we are over. We're more over than any couple have ever been. But I haven't got the energy to go into the details. He's just a pathetic, cheating, conniving . . .' I ran out of adjectives and stood there, breathing heavily and trying to come down from my hissy fit.

Shona didn't ask any more questions but said that her and Paul were going to get something to eat and then planned to spend what was left of the evening in the cinema tent and I'd better have a damn good reason for not coming with them.

Carter was waiting for me as I left the tent.

'There you are,' he said with a flash of irritation. 'I'm going to have to get you micro-chipped.'

I was in no mood to have it out with him especially as I could see the others (minus Veronique and Dylan who'd been missing in action all day) watching us. Though when I glanced over at them they all pretended that they were looking at something particularly fascinating on the ground.

I glared at Carter, throwing every ounce of hatred I felt into it. He stepped back.

'What have I done now?'

'Just stay the hell away from me,' I snapped. 'Don't talk to me, don't touch me, don't even sodding breathe near me.'

'Edie, you're being very melodramatic—' he began but I cut him off simply by flouncing over to the others while he was still in mid-sentence.

'Are we going to get something to eat or what?' I asked them and it was clear from the looks I got that Shona had filled them in on what I'd told her earlier, so they all sprang into action and spirited me off down the hill, while Carter stood there looking furious.

As we trailed aimlessly about the food stalls trying to find somewhere that didn't look too vegan or too likely to give us botulism, everyone kept a tactful silence about what had just happened between me and Carter. I could tell that Darby was dying to get all the dirt but I think Atsuko kept pinching her 'cause she kept rubbing her arm and hissing, 'What did you do that for? I wasn't going to say anything.'

We were queuing up outside the cinema tent when I saw Dylan striding towards us. Without Veronique. It was funny Carter could touch me in places that were meant to be erogenous zones and I felt nothing but the sight of Dylan in his torn Levi's and an old T-shirt reduced me to road-kill.

'Where's Veronique?' I heard Shona ask him.

'I don't know and I don't care,' was his terse reply. There was a muttered exchange between the two of them, during which I saw Dylan glance my way before he scowled, 'It's got nothing to do with me. She does what she wants, she always has. That's half the problem.' I couldn't help but wonder if he was talking about Veronique or me.

As we pushed our way into the tent, the crowd surged forwards shoving Dylan into my back and almost knocking me over. He yanked me to my feet then dropped my hand like I'd burnt him, before pointedly going over to find a space next to

Simon. And although I hadn't expected to drop Carter and pick up where I left off with Dylan I couldn't help the little pang of hurt that settled in my stomach.

27th August

That night I didn't get much sleep. In fact, it had been weeks since I'd managed a full eight hours' worth without interruptions and weird dreams. It didn't help that the ground underneath my sleeping bag was lumpy and had more stones per square inch than your average quarry. Everyone else was fast asleep which just made me feel more frustrated and lonely. And when I did finally manage to catch a few zzzzzs I was woken up by a cacophonous drumming noise outside. I pulled on my jeans and quietly clambered out of the tent.

I could hardly take in what my eyes were seeing. There were naked hippies. There were bongos. There were naked hippies making mucho noise with the bongos. I was tired, I was dirty and I had had enough.

'SHUT UP! SHUT UP!' I screamed at them. 'It's half five in the morning.'

'Hey we're just thanking the earth for welcoming us,' breezed this middle-aged guy with dreadlocks who had a huge spliff in his hand. 'Don't be so uptight, little sister.'

'You woke me up!' I yelled. 'You woke me up with your stupid bongos.'

'Here have a toke on this,' the holdover hippy suggested, brandishing the joint at me.

'I don't want it,' I protested. 'I just want you to be quiet.'

'You're the one making all the noise,' said a voice behind me. I turned round to see Dylan standing a little distance away from me with an amused look on his face. 'I was standing here listening to the bongos, as you do, when you come out of your tent and start shrieking loud enough to wake the dead.'

'Why aren't you asleep?' was all I could think of to say as the bongos started again.

'I thought I'd get up early and brave the communal showers while it was quiet,' Dylan said.

'I'd love a shower,' I breathed.

Dylan smiled evilly. 'It was nice, all that hot water and soap making me squeaky clean. And you want to know what was really amazing? When I washed my hair, I rubbed all the shampoo in and then the water sluiced it all away, all those bubbles—'

'Stop it,' I moaned.

Dylan walked over to me. 'You look awful,' he said, cupping my face in his hands. 'You still not sleeping?'

'Yeah,' I sighed.

'Listen, why don't you go and get your wash stuff and have a shower while there's no-one around and then I'll buy you breakfast and we'll watch the sun come up?' suggested Dylan.

It sounded like my idea of heaven. I nodded.

'Off you go then,' said Dylan, reaching out to ruffle my hair but I pulled away. You could have fried chips on my head. And, besides, I was all right as long as Dylan didn't touch me. It was when he touched me that things got heavy.

I never thought I'd strip off and have a communal shower. Well not since I finished school anyway and no longer had to participate in their hideous competitive sports activities. But actually there was a women's shower block and there were cubicles and the two other girls that I did see looked as embarrassed as me. As I stood under the water and scrubbed off the dirt and felt the water cascading down on me, I started to cry. I didn't even know why I was crying. I used to cry all the time. Even last year I could always be relied upon to start blubbing over silly things like a particularly harrowing episode of *EastEnders*. I was making great strides in self-control these days. But in that shower I wept like my heart was breaking. And I guess it was the strain of exams and the whole Carter thing but it was also because Dylan was outside waiting for me and although he was offering me breakfast, what I really wanted from him he wasn't able to give.

I finally emerged oozing cleanliness from every pore. It felt so good to be wearing a dress again, I'd even managed to shave my legs. Dylan was stretched out on the grass and I walked over to him and nudged him with my foot.

'I'm starving,' I said, as he sat up and looked at me. His gaze started at my feet and travelled slowly up. By the time he got to my eyes, I was trying very hard not to do something lame like go into full-on body spasms.

'You're not going to scream at me for failing to have your breakfast ready and waiting?' he asked with a slight edge to his voice.

'Not my style,' I said lightly. 'You've got the wrong girl.'

'Hmmm, if only you knew,' said Dylan significantly. He stood up and snaked his arm around my waist and I could have pulled away but it felt so right that I didn't. 'Let's get ourselves fed.'

We bought coffee and bacon rolls and sat under a tree to have breakfast and watch as the sun climbed in the sky. We didn't talk, but we didn't need to. Instead we just leant against each other and were silent. Finding someone you can be quiet with is way more difficult than sustaining a conversation. Carter used silence like a weapon but Dylan and I had always been good at companionable silences.

By this time the sun was up and staying put, it was really hot. I reached into my bag for my sunblock and started smearing it on my shoulders but Dylan took the tube from me and began to smooth the lotion onto my skin. His fingers slipped under the thin straps of my daisy-covered sun-dress and his touch became less soothing and more caressing. I held my breath as he traced a finger down my spine to the zip. Dylan hesitated for a second and then handed the tube back to me.

'You'd better do the front,' he said unsteadily.

I shoved some of the cream around my neck and arms and then turned to face him. His eyes were very green against his tan but there were dark smudges painted into the hollows of his face and I itched to smooth them away.

'I know we've had this bad patch but I really want everything to be all right between us,' I said carefully. 'And I want you to know that all the times I said I didn't want to be friends with you, I was only trying to convince myself.'

Dylan got up and tugged me to my feet so I was standing with his arms round me. 'It doesn't matter Edie,' he told me. 'I've said and done things to you that make me pretty much hate myself but you'll always be my friend. Even if I don't act that way sometimes.'

'Do you mean that?'

Dylan didn't reply but he pulled me close to him and held me. My arms crept up around his neck and he buried his head in my shoulder. I could feel his heart tapping out its beat through his thin T-shirt and I put my hand against it. Dylan gently drew back.

'I think if we're going to spend the day together we should have a no-touching rule,' he drawled in that light teasing way that I'd missed so much.

I pulled a face. 'You touched me first,' I pointed out. 'I was just returning the favour.'

'I'm serious,' Dylan insisted. 'No touching, let's just do the friend thing.'

'I never said I was going to spend the day with you,' I said jokingly and Dylan arched an eyebrow and smiled knowingly.

'Stop whining, Eeds, or I'll make you spend all morning in the trance tent.'

I really got into the whole festival vibe, man. OK, I didn't buy any stupid hats or get a henna tattoo but Dylan and I saw some bands, spent an hour in the comedy tent, pigged out on junk food and bitched about how much we hated jugglers.

Nobody knew us, nobody cared if we were dating or were friends who ended up kissing each other or even having a tempestuous affair. Being anonymous can kick some serious ass.

Dylan stuck to his no-touching rule even though our hands kept brushing and I wanted to grab his fingers and not let go. Walking round in the summer heat and not touching and the way Dylan kept looking at me like I was a Big Mac and he hadn't eaten for days made me feel restless. My whole body felt heavy and Dylan and I were exchanging so many lingering eye-meets that the whole thing was getting a bit ridiculous.

Eventually we made our way back to the tree where we'd seen the sun rise and I flopped down on the ground, exhausted.

'Next time, if I go to a festival, and it's a big *if*, I'm staying at a hotel and having myself airlifted in and out,' I announced before digging into my bag to find my emergency bottle of nail polish to start a quick repair job on my toenails that were looking decidedly chipped.

Dylan collapsed next to me, his arms pillowing his head. I tried not to look as his T-shirt rode up to reveal several inches of tanned, taut stomach.

'You're not like other girls,' Dylan said wonderingly, taking the bottle from me and hoisting my feet onto his lap so he could paint my nails. I let him. I mean what's the point of having an art boy around and not making the most of his expertise with a brush?

'How am I not like other girls?' I enquired.

Dylan shrugged. 'I don't know any other girl who'd come to a festival with a full pedicure kit and I don't know any other girl who'd put up with all the crap I've thrown at her and still want to spend time with me.'

'I've been pretty nasty to you too,' I said. 'I've said some very hurtful things.'

'I wish we could get back together now,' Dylan said casually, looking down as he concentrated on my toes. 'I think we've both changed.'

My breath caught in my throat and I couldn't speak. Was Dylan getting real or just playing 'if only' with me?

'I've thought about it a lot this summer,' Dylan continued. He paused. 'Say something, Edie. Even if it's only to yell at me.'

'I've split up with Carter,' I muttered.

'I know,' said Dylan. 'And I've tried a million times to dump Veronique but she won't listen. Or she goes mental and smashes things up.'

'So what happened outside the café wasn't a one-off?' I asked 'cause it had been something that kept tugging at my brain cells intermittently.

Dylan snorted. 'That was Veronique on a good

day. I don't even like her, let alone want to be with her, but sometimes I think we deserve each other. I try to break up with her and there are broken glasses and she threatens to hurt herself, me, her cat. It's like being back with my mum, which is just so Freudian, I don't even want to go there.'

Dylan had finished my nails now and I swung my legs off his lap and lay down, tugging Dylan with me so I could prop myself up on my elbow and look down at him.

'I have this theory,' I told him. 'I think Carter's been busy seducing me so you get the message that I'm out of bounds. Because if you're looking after Veronique then he doesn't have to.'

'I think you're spot on,' Dylan agreed. 'I've thought that for months.'

'It's so *messed*,' I said hopelessly.

'But it doesn't have to be,' Dylan said fiercely. 'If we were together and blatant about it, they'd have to let us go.'

'Rebound romances never work.'

'I only went out with Veronique to take my mind off you,' admitted Dylan. 'And when I'm with you I don't feel like I'm on the rebound, I feel like I've come home. It's like my whole world is just different combinations of black and white, but when you're around everything goes Technicolor. You're still the coolest girl I know.'

'Do you think it would work this time?' I asked hesitantly.

'It has to.' He sounded so convinced. 'My heart couldn't take being broken again.'

'So I broke your heart, did I?' I gave him a cool look. 'That's funny 'cause you broke mine too.' But it wasn't funny. I'd never told Dylan how much he'd hurt me before. And I knew that now probably wasn't the time or the place. But these things had to be said while I still had the option of walking away.

'Then we're even,' Dylan replied.

I stared at his face intently. His deep green eyes held my gaze.

'I can't go through all that again,' I told him. 'Seriously. You made me become someone I didn't like. You made me hate myself and lose sight of all the things I liked about me: my self-respect, my dignity, my honesty. You have to know that. I sort of understand why you did it, but you still treated me like shit.'

'I wouldn't put you through all that again, I promise.'

''Cause I think about us all the time, but I wonder whether we really should be together . . .' There! I'd said it. I stopped being all Tunnel Vision-girl and managed to be rational with Dylan who usually made me lose all my mental faculties.

'Edie, stop it!' Dylan exclaimed, and he gathered me up in a hug that almost threatened to break my ribs. 'You have to give me another chance. Stop trying to find reasons why it won't work before we've even started seeing each other again.'

There was so much I wanted to tell Dylan starting with the fact that I'd been in love with him for so long but there was a shadow looming over us, and I didn't mean metaphorically, as I looked up to see Carter and Veronique glaring down at us.

'What the hell is going on?' Veronique screamed.

Dylan sat up while I put my hands over my eyes in the really mature belief that if I couldn't see them, they couldn't see me.

'I'm with my best girl,' Dylan said quietly. 'What does it look like?'

'What does it look like? What does it look like?' spat Veronique. 'It looks like that little bitch has got her claws into you again.'

'Don't talk about Edie like that,' snapped Dylan, jumping to his feet.

'Look at her! She's pathetic.'

Veronique did have a point. I was still lying on the ground with my eyes covered.

Showing willing, I got to my feet. I didn't really know what to do once I was standing up,

Veronique's face was red with temper (which clashed satisfyingly with her hair), Dylan was grim-faced and Carter was smirking like he found the whole thing too entertaining for words.

'Dylan and I are getting back together,' I said eventually, more to fill up the silence than anything else. I looked to Dylan for support and he took my hand. The gesture seemed to trigger off something in Veronique. Something violent and dark and incredibly twisted.

'I didn't think sloppy seconds were your style,' she hissed at Dylan. 'You know she's been having sex with Carter for months. And he wasn't the first.'

It was as if everything had come to a standstill and the only thing moving was Veronique's mouth as all this poison spewed out of it. I let go of Dylan's hand.

'It's not true,' I whimpered, turning to Dylan. He looked like he wanted to believe me but then Carter spoke up.

'She's a real pro,' he said to Dylan in a conspiratorial way, like it was all lads together and they were down the pub. 'I can't blame you for being interested, mate.'

'Is this your revenge 'cause I wouldn't sleep with you?' I demanded as Carter turned to me with a twisted little smile.

'Edie, you seem to forget I practically had to fight you off.'

Veronique gave Dylan a triumphant look. 'I told you she was a devious little slut.'

'I'd rather be a slut than a psycho-bitch from hell,' I shouted at her, neglecting to point out that I wasn't actually a slut.

'What did you say?' she said menacingly. Dylan tried to step in between us but Veronique adroitly side-stepped him and almost as if I was watching it happen to someone else, I saw the white blur of her fist as she drove it into my stomach, which, ow, ow, OW! I yelped in pain and doubled over.

I was dimly aware of Dylan shouting and trying to take my hand but all I could focus on was the sudden nauseous waves that were threatening to drag me under.

'That's enough Veronique,' said Carter in an icy voice, as Dylan clenched his own fists.

'I haven't even started,' she promised and darted towards me. I tried to stagger out of her reach. Dylan seized her arm and told her to calm down but she twisted away from him and snatched a huge handful of my hair which she tried to use to drag me along. I started to prise her fingers away but in the end I ran with her, it was either that or lose a good chunk of my scalp. The whole thing was surreal. Dylan and Carter ran after us and begged

Veronique to leave me alone but she kept up this evil commentary about little bitches who couldn't keep their hands to themselves and I just tried to keep up with her because I didn't want her pulling my hair out by the roots.

It wasn't very Buffy-like and I so didn't want to do the whole chick-fight thing but as we approached the toilets and the crowds started thickening, Veronique had to slow down and I took the opportunity to dig my nails into her wrist. She let go of me with a curse and I pushed her away with great force. In fact I pushed her so hard that she lost her footing and slipped over the edge of the latrine pit into two days' worth of festival goers' waste product, which was being saved to use as compost.

I didn't stick around. I mean, I'd just pushed someone into a pit full of poo. There wasn't really a right way to behave after that. Still clutching my tender stomach I took off as if the hounds of hell were snapping at my feet.

By the time I got back to the tents I could hardly breathe. The others were sitting around a campfire they'd built, having a jamming session with the bongo players and they looked pretty shocked to see me come staggering towards them at great speed. For a moment I stood there, painfully winded and trying to catch my breath while they stared at me.

'You all right?' Simon asked eventually.

'I'm fine,' I gasped because it seemed easier than actually trying to explain what had just happened. 'But, hey, yeah I'm going to go home now, I think.'

'But Edie you can't,' Atsuko protested. 'We've still got two days to go.'

'No,' I sank to my knees and concentrated really hard on not throwing up. 'You don't understand; I have to go. Paul, please drive me to the nearest station. Please. Pleeease.'

'Why do you have to go home?' Shona asked, getting up and coming over to me. She looked concerned and tried to put an arm round me but I flinched away from her.

'I'm going to ruin things for everyone if I stay,' I gabbled. 'I'm fed up with me so you must be even more hacked off. Veronique and Carter told Dylan . . . they said . . . I can't stay with them here.'

I dived into my tent and started shoving things into my backpack. I could hear a muted conversation going on outside but I ignored it. And I could see someone Darby-shaped waiting for me outside, so I carefully and quietly pulled up the pegs from the back of the tent and squeezed myself and my backpack (which were roughly the same size) out of the gap I'd made and sloped off before anyone could realise that I'd gone.

Forget what I said earlier about not crying 'cause as I walked towards the side road that led off the festival site I was crying like I'd never cried before. It always amazes me how you can cry in public and people look at you in a horrified way but never actually ask you what the matter is. All those hippies were meant to be into peace and love but they obviously weren't into spreading it around. I was clutching my stomach and staggering under the weight of my backpack, all the while bawling my eyes out and not one person asked me if I was OK. Though I'd have probably told them to piss off if they had. But that's neither here nor there.

Once I'd left the site and started walking in what I hoped was the right direction for the nearest town, I had to sit down on a grass verge because I was crying so much that I was starting to get hysterical. My breath was coming and going in strange airless little gasps and my whole body felt floppy. I was also worried that I had internal bleeding from where Veronique had punched me; it certainly hurt enough. I entertained myself with fantasies that a farmer would find me dead by the side of the road and they'd have to put my name out over the radio in Florida so the 'rents could come home and bury me and Veronique would be found guilty of my murder and get sent to prison and become someone's bitch. Then I cried even harder.

Pull yourself together, Edie, I thought sternly. Deep breaths and focus. I managed to stop crying and do something useful like put my trainers on and then I hoisted my backpack onto my shoulders and began walking again.

I didn't know what I was hoping to achieve by taking off. All I knew was that I had to get home. Everything was ruined between me and Dylan – there didn't seem to be any way that he'd want to be with me now. He probably thought I was the biggest skank this side of skanktown and, besides, Veronique was definitely going to kill me if she ever saw me again. As for Carter, if I didn't see that Grade-One git for another millennium it would be too soon.

It was starting to get dark and I'd been walking for over an hour but the fields seemed to stretch out forever with no sign of civilisation in sight.

I contemplated hitch-hiking, just for a moment, but knowing my luck I'd have got picked up by some cold-eyed, cold-hearted serial killer and I had enough problems already. I walked on a bit more and was beginning to panic when I heard a car coming up behind me. I moved nearer to the hedge but it was slowing down. I turned around and raised my arm to shield my eyes from the glare of the headlights when I realised that it was the café van. My heart dipped. Dylan had come to find me! But it was Carter impatiently winding down the window and telling me to get in.

'Piss off,' I squealed and carried on trudging along the hedgerow. Carter drove alongside me.

'Get in, Edie,' he said tersely. 'It's dark and you shouldn't be out on your own.'

'Like you care,' I sniped. 'It's a bit too late for the concerned boyfriend act.'

'If you don't get in the sodding van I'm going to put you in,' he threatened, his voice simmering with barely-controlled rage.

It was either carry on walking, even though I was hopelessly lost, or get in the van with a vindictive ex-boyfriend. There didn't seem to be a lesser of the two evils option. With a bad-tempered sigh I eased off my backpack and threw it in the van, only narrowly avoiding his head, and then climbed in after it. Carter reached over and slammed the door shut before turning the key in the ignition.

'I've got better things to do with my time than drive around looking for silly little girls,' he began savagely.

'You have no right to start picking fights with

me,' I turned on him angrily. 'I don't want to talk to you, just drive me to the nearest station.'

'The nearest station is ten miles in the opposite direction,' Carter pointed out. 'I'm driving back to the site.'

'I'm not going.'

'Tough.'

I fumbled with the door-lock. 'If you don't drive me to the nearest station then I'm getting out now,' I told him, I was way beyond reason. 'Even if I have to jump out of a moving vehicle.'

'OK,' said Carter with a sigh like he was the most long-suffering person to ever exist. 'Look, I can't turn the van round, I'll carry on driving until we find a lay-by and then I—'

'Fine,' I hissed. 'And don't talk to me.'

We drove in silence. I hugged my backpack to my chest and stared out of the window at the black hedges that sped past. Of course, I couldn't keep quiet for more than five seconds.

'Why?' I finally asked. 'Why did you do it?'

Carter threw me a strangely amused look.

'Do what?' he enquired silkily.

'All of it,' I replied. 'Pretend that you liked me. Make passes at Poppy and Grace, which, by the way, was incredibly cruel of you and just this side of legal. Play twisted little mind games to try and get me into bed. Why?'

And Carter instead of coming up with one of his clever, little excuses began to laugh; a nasty, mocking laugh that seemed to echo around me.

'You're so naïve, Edie,' he eventually said. 'You think there always has to be a reason for the things people do. Maybe I did it because I'm not a very nice person.'

'No, that's not it,' I argued. 'Admit at least that you've done everything you can to keep me and Dylan apart so he can babysit Veronique which means you don't have to.'

'OK, I'll give you that,' said Carter evenly. 'Some people would call her high maintenance when she's actually just a mad cow but the rest of it, Edie, was fun. And getting to wrestle you out of your clothes, that was the most fun of all.'

My head was going to explode. Carter seemed to have turned into a Bond villain.

I opened my mouth to speak but Carter interrupted me. 'No, before you ask, I didn't have a traumatic childhood. I just like playing games with people. I mean, I always hope someone will be clever enough to see through me but you're all so bloody stupid.'

'Why did you come to find me?' I said.

'Where's the devoted Dylan, you mean?' Carter smirked. 'While everyone was running around and falling over each other to try and find you, I thought

I'd get to you first but you're being no fun, Edie. You're not playing any more, are you?'

I snorted. 'Sorry, Carter, but I'm finding it hard to see the funny in this situation.'

Carter started laughing again. 'Do you know what particularly tickled me about the whole thing?' he asked me.

'I'm sure you're going to fill me in on the details.'

'You and Dylan are meant for each other,' he informed me, his smile oozing malevolence. 'You're like, "Ooooh, no, Dylan we mustn't, our love is so tortured, we're like Manchester's answer to Romeo And Juliet."'

'I do *not* talk like that . . .'

'The pair of you are pathetic. If you loved each other, really loved each other, you wouldn't get distracted by idiotic ideas about principles and doing the right thing.'

His words were like little arrows stabbing me. He was right. I *was* pathetic. I'd been so busy trying to find reasons to stay with Carter that I'd completely ignored the obvious stuff, like that he was a twisted bastard and if I'd wanted Dylan, I should have just reached out and taken him.

'Oh, are you going to cry now, Edie?' Carter wanted to know with mock concern. 'Word of advice, sweetheart, it doesn't have any effect on me, it never did.'

Just then I saw a road sign that said 'Manor Park Hotel 50 Yards'.

'Turn in here,' I demanded. Carter ignored me and I did something I'd only seen in really bad action movies, I wrenched the steering wheel sharply to the left. Carter pushed me away with one hand.

'Are you trying to get us killed, you stupid bitch?' he roared.

'If you don't pull in now, I'm jumping out,' I warned him.

Carter swore under his breath and started to back the van down the lane and into the hotel driveway.

The Manor Park Hotel could have come straight out of a BBC costume drama. There were turrets, leaded windows and probably a few peacocks strutting about the place.

'Oh yeah, this looks like a nice little B and B,' Carter commented sarcastically as I opened the door.

It was obviously way too expensive to stay there but I figured that they'd let me phone for a cab or something. I trudged towards the main entrance where a uniformed flunky was holding the door open for me. Carter came up behind me and grabbed my arm.

'Come on Edie, stop being such a drama

queen,' he said lightly. 'Get back in the van and I'll drive you into town . . .'

'Go away,' I hissed but he wedged his hand into my armpit and tried to pull me away. 'If you don't stop I'm going to start screaming at the top of my voice,' I promised. Carter glanced at my don't-mess-with-me expression and then at the doorman who was giving him a very suspicious look.

'OK, dear,' he said, saccharine sweetly. 'If this is where you want to stay, you know I can't refuse you anything.'

I don't know what I expected once we got inside the foyer. Lots of posh people dripping in diamonds probably but instead there were lots of cute boys and cool girls. Kind of how I'd imagined the backstage enclosure of the main stage to be, if I'd actually been able to get backstage. But now wasn't the time to start wondering if that really was Professor Green.

Not with Carter still clutching my wrist in a death grip. I marched over to the reception desk to ask about ordering a cab. Before I could get the words out of my mouth, the receptionist greeted me with a warm smile. That was the first weird thing 'cause I didn't look like one of the Manor Park Hotel's regular guests or a rock star. I looked like an eighteen-year-old girl who'd been roughing it for three days. The second weird thing was when she opened her mouth.

'Hello, are you from EMI?' she enquired.

'Er, no,' I muttered.

'How much are your rooms?' Carter asked curtly.

She gave him a moderately filthy look and turned back to me with an apologetic smile. 'We're practically fully booked,' she explained. 'We've got a lot of music industry guests here for the festival.'

OK, I had been planning to get the number of a cab company but now I came to think of it the Manor Park Hotel could offer me something a whole lot better. Revenge. I bit my lip hard and tried to will my tear ducts to work as the receptionist looked at her computer screen.

'I've only got the honeymoon suite available,' she was saying. 'That would be four hundred and fifty pounds for one night, breakfast included.'

Carter made the universal 'pffft' noise for 'no bloody way'. 'Yeah right, Edie. Come on—'

I burst into loud and noisy sobs. 'Put it on your credit card,' I wept loudly as people turned to look at us. 'It's the least you could do after the terrible way you've treated me.'

Carter shifted uncomfortably; his face flushing. 'Stop it, Edie. You're making a scene.'

I cried harder. 'You tried to sleep with all my friends and now you won't even pay for a hotel room for me.'

I glanced at the receptionist from under my lashes and she gave me an almost imperceptible wink before turning to glare at Carter.

'OK, OK,' he snapped, fumbling in his pocket for his wallet and slapping his credit card down on the desk. 'I'll take the room, will you stop bawling now?'

The minute I saw her swipe his card through the till I turned off the tears and raised my eyebrows at Carter. 'Tell her to add another hundred pounds to the total for extras,' I demanded. 'I'm hungry and I need to make a transatlantic phone call.'

Carter gave me a look of utter loathing but did what I said. I waited for the receptionist to hand *me* the room key and then picked up my backpack and headed in the direction of the bar. Diet Coke first, getting rid of Carter second.

I stood next to Kate Nash as I waited to get served and tried to act nonchalantly as some of the people whose CDs I actually owned gave me strange looks. It's not every day you get to throw a full volume hissy fit in front of the cast of *TOWIE* – but I think I taught them a thing or two. I found an empty chair among a group of what looked like American rappers (I figured there was safety in numbers) and sat down to sip at my drink and decide what to do next.

But Carter was already perching himself on the edge of my chair and slinging an arm round my shoulders.

'I seem to have spent all day chasing after you,' he remarked breezily. 'You want me to push off, don't you?'

'You guessed it,' I said.

'I must say I was impressed by your little scene at reception,' he continued. 'Didn't know you had it in you. Makes me wonder what I've been missing out on.'

'What are you wittering on about now?' I said wearily.

'You,' husked Carter. 'All that passion, Edie, not to mention the deviousness. Maybe I was wrong about you. You're a girl after my own heart.'

'You wish,' I said. 'God, can you say *delusional*?'

'But you have to admit, Edie,' said Carter pretending he hadn't heard me. 'I nearly had you. Five more minutes in that tent and you wouldn't have had your precious virginity any more.'

'And then Poppy came along to save me from a fate worse than death,' I reminded him. 'Yeah, Carter, I fell for all your clever little schemes, your status as an evil mastermind is in no doubt. Now can you just sod off?'

'I'm not going anywhere,' Carter insisted, pulling me towards him. 'I've just paid five hundred and fifty pounds for the dubious pleasure of your company.'

I tried to break free of his hold but it was impossible. 'Do you really think I'm going to go upstairs with you and have sex?' I asked him incredulously. 'It's not going to happen. And anyway I've got the key.'

Carter was just about to come out with some more twisted reasoning that didn't in any way resemble our earth logic when a big American guy who was sitting near me and had been listening to our exchange with undisguised interest nudged me. I looked up expectantly waiting for the 'Is this guy bothering you?' line but instead he said, 'Honey, I think your phone's ringing.'

I looked at him blankly before remembering that my mobile was in my pack. I wrestled Carter's arm off and started burrowing for the ringing phone. By the time I found it, it had stopped ringing but Shona's number was the last one stored. I pressed Call.

She answered on the first ring.

'Edie?'

'Shona!'

'Are you OK?'

I gave Carter a sour look but he raised one

eyebrow at me and carried on sitting there. 'I'm fine. I'm sorry for taking off like that.'

'Never mind all that, give Dylan a call, he's looking for you, he was going to try and find a cab.'

'Is he mad at me?'

'He's worried about you. But if Carter's there you'd better tell him to exit sharpish, 'cause I've never seen Dylan in such a rage. Every other word that came out of his mouth began with f.'

'Oh.'

'I'll see you when?'

'Tomorrow. Hey, Shona?'

'What?'

'Guess who's standing five feet away from me?'

'I don't know.'

'Professor frickin' Green. That's who!'

'Edie, are you on drugs?'

'I'll tell you about it tomorrow.'

I cut off the call and started scrolling for Dylan's number.

'Was that your little friend Shona?' Carter taunted me. 'Wondering why they're all stranded without the van?'

'Stop acting like someone from a second-rate gangster flick. I'm calling Dylan now.'

'Oooooh, I'm really scared,' grinned Carter as I pressed Call again.

'Hey,' I said hesitantly when he answered.

'Where are you? Are you all right?'

'I'm at the Manor Park Hotel?'

I heard Dylan say something to someone.

'Dylan? Where are you?'

'I'm in a taxi, I'll be with you in about ten minutes, can you hold on?'

'Yeah, I'm fine but Carter's here and he's . . . I can't get rid of him.'

Carter looked quite chuffed about this.

'Has he hurt you?' asked Dylan.

'Oh please! Like he could but . . . just get here soon, OK?'

'I'm . . .' There was a beep and my phone cut out. The battery needed recharging. I stood up and Carter was immediately at my side.

'Going somewhere, sweetheart?' he asked.

'Dylan's on his way, he's absolutely furious with you,' I said with some satisfaction. 'Why don't you just go before there's some hideous scene?'

Carter looked unconcerned. 'I'm not frightened of *him*. He couldn't fight his way out of a paper bag.'

'Why won't you go?' I asked him tiredly.

'Give me my five hundred and fifty quid and I will,' Carter replied.

'I haven't got it,' I told him. 'And anyway I think you owe me.'

'For what? Services rendered? Hardly!'

* * *

I didn't know what to do. If I went up to the room then Carter was going to follow me and he was in such an obnoxious and confrontational mood that I wasn't entirely sure I could handle the situation. There seemed to be a lot of inappropriate touching going on. He was currently stroking my arm like it was the most natural thing in the world. But if I stayed where there were people and Dylan came in and started a fight we'd probably get thrown out. I was just wondering whether I could give Carter the slip by disappearing into the Ladies when Dylan suddenly burst through the door.

He looked awful. His eyes were deep, dark holes in an ashen face and his hair was going in fifty directions like he'd been tugging at it in desperation.

He glanced around wildly before catching sight of me and was at my side in an instant.

'Edie!' he exclaimed, running a gentle hand down my cheek. 'Thank God I found you! Why did you skip out like that?'

'It seemed like a good idea,' I admitted ruefully. 'All those things Veronique said . . .' My voice tailed off.

Dylan gave me a tiny shake. 'Like I was going to believe her! Are you all right?'

There was a cough behind us. 'I'm sorry to break

up this touching reunion,' said Carter, 'but Edie and I were just going upstairs. She forced me to book a room and, well, you know how it is . . .'

Dylan growled and lunged at Carter but I held him back.

'Look, let's all go upstairs and sort this out,' I suggested, moving towards the lift with my hand still clutching at Dylan's T-shirt so he couldn't make any sudden moves.

Carter shrugged and followed us.

The atmosphere in the lift was hostile with added bits of hostility. I stood in between Carter and Dylan as they glared at each other – the journey up to the fifth floor seemed to take an eternity.

'It's room 507,' I said absently as we walked down a thickly-carpeted corridor and Dylan smiled faintly.

'That's the room you stayed in in Paris,' he commented. Carter snorted.

Dylan stopped. 'I've just about had enough of you,' he told Carter in a cold voice that turned my insides to ice.

'The feeling's mutual,' Carter sneered. 'But I paid over five hundred quid for this room so you can either give me the money or the pair of you can sleep in the van.'

Put like that, Carter did have a point and I could see Dylan reaching the same conclusion until

Carter couldn't resist adding, 'Mind you I'd be happy to take three hundred if you threw Edie in as part of the deal.'

I jumped out of the way with a girly shriek as Dylan slammed Carter into the wall and landed him a sucker punch right on the jaw.

I didn't know who looked more surprised, Carter or Dylan. Neither of them did anything for a moment but then Carter dived at Dylan and they both went down on the floor. I stood there helplessly while they rolled about hitting each other. Dylan eventually pinned Carter to the ground and kept punching him. It was horrible. Like *When Bears Attack* on the Discovery Channel but more *When Artboys Attack*.

'Stop it!' I shouted, trying to pull Dylan off. 'Stop it, both of you!' I managed to separate them finally by grabbing an ear apiece and pinching until they were forced to stop trying to inflict maximum pain on each other. Dylan got unsteadily to his feet while Carter lay on the floor groaning, his mouth bleeding.

'I think you broke my nose,' he gasped.

'Good,' said Dylan brusquely, putting a hand up to his cheek which was starting to ooze blood where Carter had caught him with his signet ring. 'I'll break your legs if you don't leave. And if you take the van I'm calling the police to report it stolen. Now piss off and if I ever catch you within ten miles of Edie, I'll kill you.'

For once Carter had no snappy comeback. I was opening and shutting my mouth and wondering why no sound was coming out as Dylan took hold of my hand and pulled me down the corridor.

The second that we got into the room and shut the door whatever adrenalin that had been pumping through Dylan's veins seemed to evaporate and his shoulders slumped as he staggered to the bathroom. I could hear him throwing up a moment later.

Dylan was leaning over the loo on his knees as I bent down to rub his back.

'Hey Dylan,' I whispered. 'It's all right. You defeated the evil Carter monster and saved the world for, like, democracy and stuff.'

Dylan wiped his hand across his mouth and sat back on the floor. 'That was meant to be my line,' he said with a weak grin. 'That was kind of scary back there, wasn't it?'

I nodded. 'Scary to the power of one hundred,' I elaborated. 'You should have a bath or something and eat . . . we should eat . . . I'll sort that out.' And then I left the room because everything that had happened in the last hour had left me so freaked out, I was going to lose it in a pretty spectacular way if I stayed.

I curled up on the bed and thought about ringing The Mothership but knew that the minute I heard her voice, I'd revert to a mental age of three so I phoned Room Service instead and asked them to send up some food and more Diet Coke. Then I phoned Shona to let her know that the apocalypse had kind of been averted.

By that time Dylan was out of the bathroom. He seemed to have got himself under control. I was flicking through the channels on the television 'cause I might have been upset but, hey, they had all the movie channels, when he sat down on the edge of the bed furthest away from me. He was only wearing his jeans and not much else. I watched the muscles in his back shifting and gliding as he towelled his hair dry. And the reason why I was so antsy became obvious. Carter was history but now it was me and Dylan in a hotel room and the sight of his chest and the way his jeans hung low on his hips . . . I mean I could just reach out a hand and I'd be *touching him* . . .

I flung myself off the bed and reached for my bag. Dylan looked at me in surprise.

'I'm going to have a bath,' I said in the same way you might say, 'There's a plane about to crash land on our house.'

'You all right?' Dylan asked me, looking as if he thought I'd finally flipped.

'Yes!' I practically screeched. 'There's food coming, you stay here.'

And I ran bathroomwards.

I'd been immersed in bubbles for ten minutes when Dylan knocked.

'Are you sure you're all right?' he said through the door.

'You can't come in!' I yelped.

'I know.' He sounded like he was trying not to laugh. 'The food's here. They've brought champagne, on the house 'cause it's the honeymoon suite or something.'

'That's nice,' I said distractedly.

'I could sit here and chat to you if you like,' suggested Dylan still in that amused voice.

'OK,' I agreed in a small voice.

I never thought I'd have a conversation with Dylan while I was stark naked. It seemed indecent somehow even though there was a door between us. I told him what had gone down with Carter and he told me that Veronique had climbed out of the poo pit and chased him back to the tents but he'd been determined to outrun her 'cause she had muck all over her. Then she'd got changed, flung all her smelly clothes into the campfire and made Carter give her a lift to the station.

'He told me he'd taken the van without anyone knowing,' I chimed in.

'He would,' said Dylan darkly. 'We thought you were still on the site. It wasn't until later that Poppy realised you'd taken your backpack.'

'You know me, act first, think later,' I said and Dylan laughed.

'Why are you laughing?' I asked.

'It was the expression on Veronique's face when you pushed her and she realised where she was going to land,' he said in between what sounded suspiciously like giggles. I didn't know Dylan even knew how to giggle.

'Well she deserved it,' I muttered.

'I almost forgot about that,' Dylan said. 'Is your tummy all right?'

I looked at my stomach through the bubbles, it looked like there was a big cloudy bruise emerging on the surface. 'It's a bit tender,' I replied. 'How do you know if you have, like, internal bleeding?'

There was a pause and then Dylan said in such a sultry voice that it made my toes curl, 'Hmm, I'll have to have a look at that later.'

I looked up at the ceiling and then slid under the water where I didn't have to think about the ramifications of what he'd said.

I'd just finished rinsing the conditioner out of my

hair when Dylan knocked on the door. 'Have you drowned?'

'I'll be out in five minutes,' I said, although part of me wanted to stay in there all night and the other part of me wanted to get the hell out of there and jump Dylan's bones.

Conflict, thy name is Edie.

I pulled on my pink spotty pyjama bottoms and a black camisole vest which were the only clean clothes I had left and forced myself to open the door.

Dylan was sprawled on his stomach on the bed, still wearing just his jeans, and sipping champagne.

He gave me a lazy smile. 'Hey you,' he said softly.

'Hey yourself,' I murmured, hitching up my pyjama bottoms as they settled on my hips. Dylan looked at me with interest.

'Do you need a hand there?' he asked, arching an eyebrow provocatively.

'I'm having elastic problems,' I scowled, circling the bed warily. Maybe I could sit on a chair. In fact, maybe I could sleep on a chair but Dylan patted the bed. It looked very inviting. *He* looked very inviting.

'C'mon, I won't bite,' he was saying. There was another pause. 'Well, not unless you want me to.'

'Stop being so, so . . . seductive,' I bit out crossly,

climbing onto the bed and making sure I kept a safe distance away from him.

Dylan stretched out an arm and pulled the food trolley nearer.

'Do you want something to eat?'

I considered the question. I couldn't kiss him if I was eating. But then were we going to be kissing? It seemed like we were getting to the point where kissing was going to be entirely necessary.

'There's chips,' Dylan said cajolingly. 'They're still hot.'

I scrambled towards him and investigated dinner then sat cross-legged while I ate chips and drank champagne. It was so decadent. Dylan rolled onto his back and watched me as I washed down the rest of the chips with what was left in my glass.

'So you've finished eating, what are we going to do now?' he wanted to know as I stole a hungry glance at the way his chest rose as he spoke.

I lay down next to him, keeping a foot of bed between us and figured I might as well try and get some sleep. But it was like that thing you do when you clasp your fingers together and try to keep your thumbs apart. Slowly but surely our bodies inched towards the middle of the bed and then I could feel Dylan's arm pressing against my side. It seemed to burn where it touched me.

I gave a desperate groan and flung myself on

top of him. Dylan was very obliging as I wound myself around him, I wanted to bury myself inside him. I smothered his face in kisses; his forehead, his eyelids, his cheeks and then I bit his lower lip gently between my teeth.

That was my undoing. Dylan suddenly moved so I was trapped beneath him and he caught my mouth in a deep kiss. My lips parted as he traced the contours of my mouth with the tip of his tongue before plunging inside.

They were long, languorous kisses that tasted of hot summer afternoons. But then Dylan moaned into my mouth and I couldn't help but arch up against him and everything changed. Became fiercer and faster and inevitable.

We toppled off the bed onto the floor, clothes getting tugged away, both of us desperate not to lose contact with the other. Dylan ran a hand down my body.

'Mine,' he said possessively. 'You're mine. I've always loved you, even when I thought I'd lost you.'

I stroked his face. 'I love you too,' I told him. The words sounded strange, I'd never said it out loud before and meant it so much. 'When we were in Paris, you stopped being a crush . . .'

Dylan smoothed the hair back from my face. 'We don't have to, if you don't want to.'

I put a finger to his lips. 'I do. But, you know, I'm still . . . it's my first time. I didn't, not with him. I think I always wanted it to be you.'

Dylan smiled and nipped at my finger. 'I wanted it to be me too,' he admitted. 'I'll be gentle, I promise.'

As I slid between the covers I wondered why I wasn't panicking like I had been with Carter and I realised it was 'cause it felt right. Right place, right time and definitely the right boy.

Dylan hesitated before getting back into bed. 'Edie?'

'Hmmm?' I said dreamily tracing a finger down his back. Dylan caught my hand and pressed a kiss into my palm.

'Have you got any . . . I haven't got any protection,' he said with an embarrassed smile.

'In my backpack,' I murmured. 'I've got about fifty condoms.' And then I started laughing.

'What's so funny?' Dylan asked, almost falling out of bed as he dragged my backpack across the floor.

'I never thought when I bought them that I'd actually be using them, y'know, in a room like this and with *you*!' I said, giggling.

'I'm glad you *are* using them with me,' Dylan said slightly huffily. 'And not with Carter.'

'If you're trying to kill the moment by talking

about that wanker, then you're going the right way about it,' I pouted.

Dylan gave a smile that was positively evil and rolled on top of me. 'You're so sexy when you get stroppy,' he purred. 'Which is practically all the time.'

'Oh, shut up.'

Then Dylan was kissing me hard and it was all I could do to remember to breathe. And when it finally happened Dylan held me tight and whispered sweet things in my ear. His fingers traced patterns all over me as he touched my skin wonderingly as if he couldn't believe that I was there and we were doing what we were doing. Afterwards, he folded me up in his arms and kissed my forehead and told me how much he loved me.

When I woke up the first fingers of light were beginning to creep through the curtains. Dylan was asleep, his arm around my waist. I lay there for a minute trying not to think but it was no good. There was too much stuff going on in my head and I really needed to pee.

I wriggled out of bed and hunted for some clothes. I might have had sex (oh my God, I'd *had* sex!) but I wasn't ready to strut around bare-ass naked. I found Dylan's T-shirt and pulled it on before scurrying into the bathroom.

While I was washing my hands, I looked at myself in the mirror. My face stared back. Same old Edie. Same old fringe that wouldn't lie flat. Same old blue eyes. Same old freckles. Same old slightly-too-pouty mouth. I'd read these books where after the heroine had lost her virginity she'd go look in the mirror and realise she'd turned into a woman. But, y'know, not so much. I still looked Edie-shaped. Though I felt a bit wobbly still. I hadn't like, *come* but the feeling of closeness, the feeling that me and Dylan were together, like, really, really together had been wonderful and a tiny bit frightening at the same time. Yawning, I crept back into bed and Dylan gave a sigh and pulled me against him.

'What are you wearing?' he complained sleepily.

'Your T-shirt,' I sighed, fighting between my modesty and how nice it felt to have Dylan's chest pressed against my back. Niceness won and I tugged off the offending item.

'That's better,' said Dylan, sounding more awake. He kissed my shoulder.

'I've missed you.'

'I only went to the bathroom,' I protested.

'No, I mean I missed you when we weren't together,' Dylan replied. 'I missed your smile and your freckles and your Edieisms and I missed you.'

I turned round so I was facing him. 'I missed you too but I always knew we'd get back together,' I said firmly.

'Was it all right before?' Dylan asked, wrapping his arms round me. 'I didn't hurt you, did I?'

'It was fine,' I told him. 'It wasn't like how I imagined it.'

Dylan frowned. 'It gets better. I tried to take it slow.'

I smiled. 'I didn't mean it like that.' I traced his lips with my finger. I loved the fact that he was mine to touch again. 'Isn't it strange? Sex, I mean. It's just so odd. Majorly odd.'

Dylan laughed, his eyebrows quirking upwards, a wicked look on his face. 'Pity to let this bed go to waste.'

'We could always go back to sleep,' I suggested with a smirk.

'But I had something else in mind,' he drawled.

And the second time was different to the first. Better. Infinitely, wonderfully better. Then I slept in Dylan's arms until someone tapped on the door and told us we had to check out in half an hour. I'd been scared that when I woke up, the dream would have disappeared but it was still there. Dylan was still there.

We drove back to the site even though I was

contemplating emptying my bank account so we could spend another night at the Manor Park.

'Hmmm, it was sort of cool in a so-chintzy-it-made-my-eyes-hurt way,' agreed Dylan sarcastically when I put the idea to him, but he started up the van anyway.

I narrowed my eyes at him. 'It's not the decor I like. It's the fact that it doesn't resemble a tent.'

'You're *such* a princess,' laughed Dylan. 'But I do have a vacancy in my two-man tent that you might be interested in.'

'I wonder what the others will think,' I mused.

'I don't care,' said Dylan decisively. 'I don't care about anything except you. Do you know what I thought last night when you were asleep and I was holding you?'

'What?' I asked in a trembly voice.

'That you and me were inevitable. You're the only thing that makes me happy.'

'You make me happy too,' I admitted. 'But it's not like last time, I don't think. 'Cause I'm way more mature than you now.' Dylan rolled his eyes at that. 'And I don't think it's about being friends and kissing each other. We're, like, having a relationship.'

'I can handle it, if you can,' grinned Dylan. 'You game?'

I reached out a hand and gently pulled at his hair. 'If you break my heart again, I'm going to kill you,' I said quietly.

Dylan pulled me across the seat and wrapped an arm around me. I rested my head against his shoulder.

'It's not going to happen,' he promised. That was good enough for me.

I could hear the steady beat of his heart and smell the scent of lemons and soap on his skin. Dylan sang along to an old song on the radio, one hand resting lightly on the steering wheel, and the road stretched out before us.

This piece was originally written to accompany *Diary of a Crush* the first time it was published as a trilogy, which was way back in 2004.

Edie's Twelve Degrees of Crushing

Hello, Edie here.

Now, I might not be the class brainiac, but there are some things I'm an expert in. Like, buying vintage frocks on Ebay or the fifteen different ways to eat a Twix. And the one subject that I get an A plus in every time, is the ancient art of crushing. I crush, therefore I am.

I've decided to share the benefit of my wisdom and after months of hopelessly lusting after Dylan, I've REALISED that there are twelve degrees of crushing from the slightly embarrassing things most girls will do to catch the eye of the heir to their heart, to the verging on ridiculous stunts you pull when you're in the grip of a passion that renders you powerless. And then there are the other things – the deranged, insane things that will probably result in you being sectioned or sent to your room until you're thirty.

I've written it all down in a handy list. No need to thank me.

Low-level love stuff

1. *Weirdy compatibility stuff*
It's not enough to simply like the look of someone. You have to know that it's meant to be. That you both can't function without three hits of sugar in your coffee or that you both look really good in green. Or, gasp, you both love quoting funny bits of *Modern Family*.

Sometimes you need science to prove your compatibility, which is why I spend a lot of time working out my love percentage (www.atombooks.net/books/love-calculator), I can then bore my friends and my cat by informing them that, 'Yay! We love each other 98%!'

2. *Having a working knowledge of his schedule*
How the hell else will you know exactly what bus your beloved gets to and from his place of learning? And you can tell so much about a boy by knowing that he always goes to Pizza Express on a Saturday afternoon, can't you?

3. *Trying out his surname*
Just so you know whether to keep your own name

when you get married or whether you'll actually like the way Mrs Shovelbottom sounds.

4. *Thinking of excuses to talk to him*

Stick to the weather, telly and how much coursework sucks. Don't make the mistake of spending too long thinking of something to say. 'Cause when you do pluck up the courage to like, talk to him, you'll end up saying something completely hatstand. 'Do you like *Glee*?' will come out as 'Kurt! Quinn! Unk! Unk!' leaving your love-god with a look of bewilderment on his face. Not all attention is good attention.

Mildly alarming amour antics

5. *Obsessing over stuff he's touched*

About a month into your crush (if no-one tastier has come along) you'll find that you've amassed a small collection of bizarre white elephants and *objets d'art*. Let's take a look, shall we? A couple of old Coke cans, a balled-up sheet of Italian vocab, an empty Doritos bag and, best of all, a sweaty footie shirt that you, erm, found when he left his bag unattended in Starbucks. What have all these items got in common? Why, they've all known the touch of his heavenly hands, like you didn't already know that.

6. *Special coded communications*

Although you and your mates all know the true identities of your respective crushes, it would never do to mention them by name. Instead you create a new way of communicating with each other. Why? Because the world would end if anyone were to hear you discussing the pert pecs of Trent the art supply shop assistant. Instead you say things like, 'Artboy has arm bumps. Over.' Should come in handy if there's ever an opening at MI6.

7. *Planning to bump into him*

It's not enough that you might just happen to bump into him. You plan every potential encounter with your special boy like a military campaign. For starters, you've already memorised his weekly movements so you have a pretty clear idea of when and where he'll be. You also spend hours designing a look that suggests you've just happened to throw on the nearest outfit. But then when you do track him down, you're too freaked out by his nearness to do anything but run away.

8. *Copying out his telephone number in your best handwriting and keeping it with you at all times.* Even though if you lost your phone, you could never forget his number – it's engraved on your heart!

Brrrrrrring! Brrrrrrring. Stalker alert!

9. *Finding out his home phone number, and calling it 24/7*
Because when he picks up the phone and says, 'Hello, 4436988', it makes your heart turn somersaults. And if you dial 141 before tapping in his number he can never trace your call. Well, not until his family get the police involved, that is.

10. *Curtain twitching*
In your heart of hearts you know that one day your crush will suddenly wake up, realise that you're his and knock on your front door to sweep you off on the best date ever, ever, EVER. Until that happy day, you spend your life stealthily peering out at your street from the front room window, just in case the doorbell rang while you were doing noisy stuff like running water or shouting at your tiresome little brother.

11. *Analysing everything*
When he says, 'Hi' to you after you 'accidentally' crashed your bike against his, you begin to wonder what he meant. And why did his voice go slightly up in pitch at the end of the syllable? And did he raise one of his eyebrows half a millimetre higher than the other one? And if he did, what was he trying to tell you? Why? Why? Why?

12. *Walking up and down outside his house*
You sad, sad girl. Stop it right now.

Turn the page for a sneak peek
at the next instalment
from Edie's journal:

Sealed With a Kiss

Manchester – America – London
Edie's Diary Volume 3

I can't believe that my diary now has volumes! I'm, like, a twenty-first century Samuel Pepys or possibly someone less old, uncool, male and, y'know, *dead* who also kept a diary.

Anyway, my life up till now has been girl (that would be me), meets boy (that would be Dylan) and then fast forward through two years of torturous back and forth, kissing and fighting and all points in between. And now it's all different. Dylan and I have been back together for nearly a month and we've managed not to have a single argument. Weird. Carter (the king of evil ex-boyfriends) is still seething in the background but thankfully there have been no sightings of Veronique (his sister and the queen of evil ex-girlfriends).

And the other less-Dylan-y, but just as important parts of my life involve working in a café, being in a band with my friends, Poppy, Atsuko and Darby, and trying to decide what I want to be when I finally grow up.

12th September

Dylan and I haven't done it for two weeks. Having the parents back from their second honeymoon thing is kinda cramping my style.

There's, like, nowhere to go that doesn't involve secluded corners of parks or spending vast sums of money on a hotel room. And although the getting pelvic is fantastic, I kinda enjoy all the furtive kissing that doesn't lead anywhere.

Sex is strange. It's like this big secret that I have that no-one else knows about. Like this place that only Dylan and me have been to. Before the 'rents came home, he spent all his time here. And we'd just disappear under my covers, popping out now and then to load up with supplies from the fridge. It's not like we were doing it all the time, because we weren't, but the rest of the world just slipped away until all there was was Dylan and me. And what we used to be is nothing like what we've become.

When it's dark and the only light is coming from the muted television set in the corner of my bedroom, he talks in whispers about everything. His family and his dreams and what makes him frightened. Most of which I'm not going to put down here 'cause it's private – it's Dylan's story, not mine. But it made me understand why he is like he is, which is moody and difficult and messed up but still the sweetest boy you could ever hope to meet.

And did I mention the part where I fall in love with him a little bit more every day? It's a lot like drowning but the water feels so warm and wet against my skin that I don't really mind.

14th September

We had another band rehearsal tonight. We're starting to sound like a proper group. If proper groups sang songs about pink Converse All-Stars and had a lead singer who insisted on hula-hooping during the fast songs. Poppy is becoming more and more of a mentalist every day, which leads me to the part where me and Atsuko and Darby were just packing away our gear when Poppy suddenly dropped her bombshell. 'Oh by the way,' she announced casually. Way too casually. 'We're playing a gig next month. On Halloween actually.'

'What?!' we screamed in unison.

'What's the what?' she asked innocently. 'There's no point in rehearsing forever. We're ready for a paying audience.'

'But, but, but . . .' stammered Darby while Atsuko narrowed her eyes and began cursing under her breath in Japanese. That is, I think they were swear words, I couldn't be entirely sure.

Poppy began to twitch. 'Is that the time? Gotta go.' Then she practically ran out of the room though she'd never admit that she was too chicken to stay and face her band-mates' wrath.

'I'm so going to kill your sister,' I told Grace as we walked to the chippy later.

Grace didn't look too perturbed. 'She's just impulsive,' she said in her tiny voice. Since we got back from the festival, Grace and I have become mates. Well, I talk and she listens. I think the whole having-her-Highland-Spring-spiked-with-acid incident made her realise that she actually had to take part in life, instead of just observing it from the sidelines. Since then I've made a point of trying to drag her out of her shell. Because I'm all heart, in case you hadn't noticed.

As we reached the top of her road, my mobile started ringing. It was Dylan.

'Hey you,' I said softly.

'All my flatmates have disappeared off to Altrincham for an all-night rave,' Dylan drawled.

'And?' I prompted.

'Fancy a sleepover?'

'Cool! Shall I bring DVDs and ice cream?' I enquired.

'Just bring yourself and your toothbrush,' Dylan purred. 'And I'll provide the entertainment.'

Yay! I'm going to get seduced tonight. Go team Edie!

15th September

What I like about staying over at Dylan's:

1. He has a proper double bed, even though he chooses to encroach on my half of it.
2. He always wakes me up with a kiss and a cup of coffee.
3. The smoochies part of staying over gets better and better.
4. Even though they're a pikey student household, they have a far more expensive cable package than we do at home so we can watch Bollywood films till really late and make up the dialogue.
5. Dylan's there.

What I don't like about staying over at Dylan's:

1. Communal bathroom with no power shower, toilet seat always *up* and Carter barging in (the flimsy lock was no match for the arrogant way he flung the freaking door open without knocking) while I was cleaning my teeth.

Luckily I was clothed. 'Cause I learnt pretty quickly that you don't wander round in your underwear when your boyfriend lives with other boys.

I glared at Carter, but it was pretty hard to pull off when I had a mouthful of toothpaste, which was threatening to dribble down my chin.

'Oh, you stay over now, do you?' Carter enquired with a nasty smile. 'God, you've gone from shy virgin to experienced woman of the world in sixty seconds.'

I spat a big mouthful of foam into the basin and pointed at the door with my toothbrush. 'Get out!'

But Carter just stood there, grinning like the total, toxic cretin that he is. 'You know something, sweetheart?' he said in a low, confiding tone, leaning closer to me. 'You're not looking as cottony fresh as you used to. In fact, you seem a bit worn-in, a bit pounded, if you get my drift.'

I took a step back to get away from him and got banged in the butt by the edge of the sink. 'Firstly, ew! And secondly, get the *hell* out!' I said furiously, but I kept my voice down because if Dylan knew that Carter had come into the bathroom while I was in there, let alone knew what he'd just said to me, it would have been like the Iraqi Conflict all over again. But with art boys.

I made another threatening gesture with the hand that was brandishing my toothbrush and with that stupid, inane chuckle of his, Carter finally got out.

It left me in a bad mood for the rest of the day.

19th September
Dylan'll be going back to university at the end of this week. That means no more smooching in the storeroom 'cause he's also starting back at his regular part-time job in Rhythm Records next door.

'It's a good excuse to have a party this weekend,'

Poppy pointed out as I bemoaned the disadvantages of not having a willing kiss-object at my beck and call.

'Well it would make a nice break from the chip fat in here and being in a band with a complete slave-driver who wants me to rehearse twenty-four seven,' I agreed.

'It's just over a month to go till our gig,' Poppy reminded me yet again. 'We have to be perfect. In a really cool, rock 'n' roll kind of way.'

I waved my hands in front of her face. 'Between mastering A flat diminished and the endless washing-up, my fingers are seizing up. I'm going to start charging you for my hand-cream supplies.'

'Stop being a drama queen and go and take this order to table five.'

I'm sure I'm developing calluses on the tips of my fingers from all that strumming action. Plus I have to have really short nails now and the polish just gets scraped off as soon as I apply it. This rock 'n' roll stuff is not in the least bit glamorous.

21st September

If I thought I could spend the next year waiting tables while waiting to be famous, The Mothership has other ideas. She's got this notion that I should spend my gap year doing something worthy (translation: *boring*) like working in the Third World or going trekking in the

Hindu Kush. What she really means is that she doesn't like me going out with Dylan. Not when I could be having a proper, committed relationship with the 'lovely Jake'.

'Carter was an evil, scheming rat,' I told her till I was blue in the face.

'Well he had charming manners,' my mum said mildly. 'While Dylan, well he's very glowery, isn't he?'

Jesus!

22nd September

I took the day off so I could spend some quality time with Dylan before he becomes re-immersed in doing art boy stuff.

We went to the Tate Modern in London and after we'd admired the Warhols we walked hand in hand by the Thames, which isn't a patch on the Manchester Ship Canal, quite frankly.

'I hate that summer's over,' I moaned as we sat down on a bench. 'There's absolutely nothing to look forward to.'

'Winter's good too,' said Dylan. 'We can stay in and I'll paint while you play the guitar and it'll be all dark outside.'

And where was the fun in that? 'Yeah, but your central heating doesn't work,' I reminded him, thinking back to a party they'd thrown last winter when I'd had to keep my coat on for, like, the entire three hours I was there.

Dylan grinned and shook his head at me. 'You're such a princess.'

'My mum doesn't think so.' I rested my head against his shoulder because that's my head's preferred resting place these days. 'She thinks I should be travelling round Asia in my gap year. Like, I would ever go anywhere that doesn't have public lavatories. *Clean* public lavatories.'

'We could go somewhere next summer,' Dylan said but I thought he was trying to get me off the topic of public conveniences.

'Like where? Blackpool? Or, hey, maybe we could go back to Paris at a push.'

Dylan gave a start and I had to sit up. 'Oh! Yeah! We should go to America.'

'Dream on, D. It would cost a fortune.' I stood up and stretched lazily. 'But my limited funds will stretch to a couple of ice creams.'

'It wouldn't have to cost that much. I have some money in the bank from the guilt fund my dad left me when he walked out anyway,' Dylan continued, leaning forward and yanking me back down on the bench. 'If we went next summer we'd have a whole year to save up and we could hire a car and do a road trip. Road trip, Eeds!'

I still wasn't convinced. 'So you think we'll still be together then?' I asked him.

He touched my face lightly. 'You don't get rid

of me that easily.' He moved closer to me and brushed my mouth with his. 'Just think, we could go to New York, LA, San Francisco . . .' He nudged me with his elbow. 'You know you want to.'

He was right. I did. I wanted us to stay together and I wanted to do stuff with him. Exciting, adventurey stuff like going on a road trip in a cool car and going to places that I'd only seen in films. And shopping. A girl could do some serious shopping in the land of rampant consumerism.

'Well I have always wanted to go to New Orleans,' I admitted carefully. 'And Seattle, maybe Chicago, oooh! And we *so* have to go to Las Vegas! Oh God, we're going to do this, aren't we? We're going to do a road trip and I'm going to save all my tips and empty out my Marc Jacobs shoe savings account . . .'

Dylan jumped up so he could pull me to my feet, hoist me up and swing me round till I squealed because I was getting dizzy. 'Think of all those cheap motel rooms too! Double beds, no parents, no friends, no annoying flatmates.'

'Talking of which my parents have got a do tonight.'

Dylan smirked and leered at me at the same time, which was quite a feat. 'So that means . . .'

'An empty house. C'mon let's go and get the train home.'

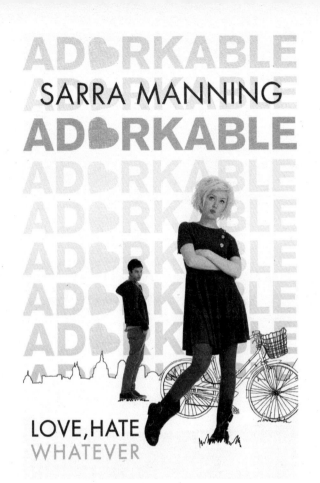

ADORKABLE

SARRA MANNING

ADORKABLE

LOVE, HATE
WHATEVER

Jeane Smith's a blogger, a dreamer, a dare-to-
dreamer, jumble sale queen, CEO of her own lifestyle
brand and has half a million followers on Twitter.

Michael Lee's a star of school, stage and playing
field. A golden boy in a Jack Wills hoodie.

They have nothing in common but a pair of cheating exes. So why can't they stop snogging?